I0626233

LEONIE
GANT

CURSE

THE

TRUTH

The Harstone Legacy
Book 5

Copyright © 2020 Leonie Gant

No part of this publication may be reproduced, distributed, or transmitted in any form or by any means, including photocopying, recording, or other electronic or mechanical methods, without the prior written permission of the publisher, except in the case of brief quotations embodied in critical reviews and certain other noncommercial uses permitted by copyright law.

This novel is a work of fiction. Names, characters, businesses, places, events, and incidents are the product of the author's imagination or used in a fictitious manner. Any resemblance to actual persons, living or dead, or actual events, is purely coincidental.

ISBN-13: 978-0-6489811-1-4

To Mike, Samuel and Nicholas.

*U*sually, when you have an earth-shattering secret that could lead to your untimely demise if discovered, you do everything you can to keep it quiet. My aunt, the leader of the witch's coven I belonged to, was advocating something a little different.

"Have you completely lost your mind?"

Those were the words of a berserker werewolf sheriff who was also subject to a Destined Beloved prophecy. As that meant he was supposedly my soul mate with all the emotional upheaval that entails, he was not coping well with my aunt's proposal.

"You want to announce to the whole town that Sadie is a cursebreaker, even though you know it has a death sentence attached to it."

"Or we could go with your brilliant suggestion which is to hide her away so she's on the run her entire life."

I never knew my aunt had that level of snark to her.

Flora drew in a deep breath as if trying to calm herself. "Bad things happen in the dark. If nobody knows her secret and the Conclave comes after her, she disappears and is just another unfortunate missing woman. If everybody knows who and what she is, we might be able to protect her. The Conclave is not going to want to resume a genocide in this day and age when everybody is watching," she insisted.

Personally, I thought she was underestimating how evil governing bodies could be, but the paranormal world, and witch politics in particular, were her domain. She had done everything she could to protect me so far. I wasn't going to start second guessing her instincts now.

"I'm quitting as sheriff," Conall announced. "That way I can protect you twenty-four hours a day without any distractions."

My head snapped up. I did not like that idea at all. Sheriff Conall Tolan was unbearably overprotective on a good day. If he wasn't distracted by the criminal element of the small paranormal town of Walker Bay, I might get to the point where I cheerfully smothered him in his sleep.

"That's not happening."

Amusing as it was to watch two of the most powerful beings I was ever likely to meet going head to head and seeing who would crack first, I'd finally reached the point where I needed to step in. I had been fine with letting them wear themselves out arguing over my future, and then I planned to step in and tell them what was going to happen, but the prospect of no break from the protectiveness of my Destined Beloved was more than I was willing to accept.

"You know, if you married me it would give you an extra level of protection. Not many would be willing to take on the Tolan name."

For the love of... "Will you stop demanding that I marry you." This was beginning to get irritating.

Three months ago, I didn't know that Sheriff Conall Tolan existed. At that stage I didn't know that werewolves existed, or witches, or ogres, or centaurs, or trolls. Now I did know. I knew that my father had been a witch who'd had a one-night stand with my mother, thus giving me the curse-breaker genes which were causing all this hassle. I knew that the Seer was able to have a Destined Beloved prophecy which linked your soul with somebody you barely knew, even if neither of you were prepared for the relationship. I also now had an intimate knowledge of the way that true evil looked, the sort of evil willing to sacrifice friends, neighbors and their children in the interests of ambition, rage and hate.

"Anyway, your father would be the first to hand me over."

Conall's relationship with most of his family could best be described as strained, and that animosity had spilled over to me. I wasn't exactly sure how much protection we'd get from that quarter.

I could see the worry in Flora's eyes, and I knew that she liked the idea of me marrying Conall. Three weeks ago, our relationship had been fine, but we'd hit a little bump in our road to happily ever after. Conall had started wondering whether the Destined Beloved prophecy was a magical trap that he'd been caught in. Being an alpha male with some relationship issues courtesy of his family life, he'd decided to break all contact with me for a couple of weeks while he was on a work trip to see if what he had were real feelings or whether he could put them aside. Unfortunately, he'd neglected to inform me about what he was doing, so I thought I'd been ghosted by the man I was beginning to care about, for the second time in my life. He came back determined that he loved me and wanted to marry me. I wasn't quite as receptive to his revelation as he had hoped. To be frank, I was pretty annoyed at the way he had gone about things. He wanted me to forgive him and accept a marriage proposal. I wasn't quite there yet.

"We're going with Flora's plan to announce what I am. The secret is already out. We have no idea who has the video of me breaking Tilda's curse. We need to get in front of this thing."

The day before, my closest friend had been attacked by the man she had been dating. He put a curse on her to flush me out by forcing me to use my abilities. He'd filmed what I did and, despite being captured, we had no idea who was currently in possession of that footage. Liam Rigby had been a magister of the Conclave which was the ruling body for witches. Chances were that was where that footage had ended up.

"You do realize there are still two magisters in this town," Conall pointed out. "They would be duty bound to take you into custody if you were outed as a cursebreaker. The precepts of the Conclave are clear. There is a death sentence on the head of every cursebreaker and, considering they managed to wipe all of them out centuries ago, they're pretty effective at carrying that precept out. Bernauer is not going to protect you, and Hartford will think all her Christmases have come at once."

Julian Bernauer was my ex-boyfriend who had taken off after I told him I loved him, months before I found out about the paranormal world. You can imagine my surprise when he turned up in Walker Bay as a magister, tasked with investigating the curses that had been cast by rogue witches. I had never known he was a witch. I was also shocked to find out he had been engaged as a child in an arranged marriage, and that his fiancée was also a magister. I could definitely imagine the joy on Penelope Hartford's face if she discovered I was a cursebreaker. Especially as Julian was currently in the process of breaking off the engagement due to his professed goal of convincing me to ditch the Destined Beloved prophecy and going back to him. I scrubbed my hands over my face. If there was any clear lesson to be gained from this mess, it was never get involved with a magister.

I grasped Flora's hands and looked her directly in the eyes. "I trust your instincts and I agree. I can't protect this town from what seems to be happening if I have to keep this secret as well."

Flora nodded sharply. "I'll organize a town meeting. There's no point in just telling the coven. If we want protection in numbers, everybody needs to know the truth."

2

↑

*Y*ou would have thought I'd have learned by now never to underestimate my aunt's organizational abilities. It only took her a few hours to pull together a meeting of the entire Town Council, and that included the time it took to convince Aidan Tolan, the leader of the werewolf clan, who was happy to fight anything Flora wanted on principle. As I took my seat at the front of the hall and watched a large number of the town wander in, I was gripped by a sudden doubt. This was it. We were announcing to Walker Bay that I was a cursebreaker. I wish I had more confidence that this was going to go well. I understood the reasoning behind this decision and considering my only other option was to run and hide, I didn't have a choice. Still, this was a big and possibly very ugly step.

"You're contemplating running, aren't you?"

I glanced up as my friend, Tilda, slid into the seat next to me. I pulled a troll doll out of my bag and activated the privacy spell that was attached to it.

"That's just one of the options going through my head at

the moment," I muttered. "I'm just worried about how this is going to be received."

Tilda lifted an eyebrow. "We already know how it's going to be received. There will be some people who stick by your side, some people who won't care, and then there will be the rabid few who want your head on a spike."

I already had a pretty good idea who the rabid few were going to be, and few was probably an understatement.

"None of that means anything," Tilda continued. "What's important is that everybody will know what you are. Hopefully, that spotlight will prevent the Conclave from doing something stupid."

That something stupid was having me killed because, and I couldn't believe this was true in this day and age, being a cursebreaker carried an automatic death sentence. That law hadn't been used in hundreds of years, thanks to the fact that the Conclave had been so successful in wiping out all the cursebreaker families. I was going to be the test case to see how civilized the world had become over the last several hundred years. Wasn't that a cheery thought?

"How many do you think are going to want to turn me over immediately?" I asked as I looked around.

Tilda screwed up her face. "I'd say around a hundred."

I was shocked. "A hundred? Where did you pull that number from?"

"Well, the Path coven is going to use it as a way to hit Flora, the werewolves will be thrilled to see you go down because they blame you for sending Brian Tolan to jail."

"He was the one murdering people," I reminded her.

Tilda looked at me with a sympathetic expression. "I can't believe that after almost three months here, you still think the facts matter."

I was about to reply when Deputies Karl Iversen and Beastpike took up seats flanking the both of us.

"What are you doing?" Pike asked, leaning back in his chair as if he didn't have a care in the world.

Tilda grinned at the way the dwarf was trying to portray a casual air. For the record, it wasn't working. He still looked like he'd be happier in the middle of a bar brawl. "We're trying to work out who is going to want to have Sadie handed over to the Conclave. I'm thinking of turning it into a game of bingo. You know, as each one stands up."

Karl shook his head. "You two have a sick streak to you, you know that, don't you?"

Pike looked as if he was contemplating the situation. "If you think about it, this is going to be one way of finding out who the crazies in town are. You know, the ones who are willing to turn on their neighbors, regardless of the immorality of the law in question."

I was beginning to think that my friends were not taking this situation as seriously as I believed it warranted.

"Move."

I should have known that my Destined Beloved would not leave my side for long. Since I had made the decision to go public, he had become more overprotective and crankier than he had been before.

Karl raised an eyebrow. "You're going to need to take it down a notch, Sheriff," he warned. "People are already twitchy enough about an unexpected meeting being called. It won't help if they think their sheriff is going to go full berserker on them."

Nobody wanted to see that. Ever since the sheriff had been outed as a berserker, there had been a certain wariness in the town's treatment of him. As the person who had most often seen the sheriff in that state, I could confirm that the sight was just as horrifying as the town feared.

Conall didn't say a word. He just stood there waiting until Karl sighed and shuffled over, leaving the seat beside me free.

The sheriff sat down and grasped my hand. I looked down at where my hand was entwined with his, noting the white knuckled grip he had on me.

I leaned over and whispered in his ear. "I'm fine, I'm not worried." Sure, I was lying, but I knew that he wasn't fond of this plan.

Conall turned and my breath caught at the intense fear in his eyes. "Who says I'm doing this for you? I need to know you're close and somebody can't rip you away from me."

He turned away and stared straight at the stage. I lowered my head onto his shoulder.

"Nobody's going to take me away," I said, trying to inject a confidence into my voice that I didn't necessarily feel.

Next to me I felt Tilda elbow me in the ribs.

"What…?" I looked up and saw what the problem was.

Conall's brother, Eamon, was glaring at Pike who was ignoring him completely. Maybe not completely. He had an evil grin on his face that told me he knew he was messing with the werewolf, and he was enjoying every minute of it. It seemed Eamon had professed to Tilda that he was madly in love with her after she was almost killed by her boyfriend. Aside from having appalling timing, Eamon was also the eldest son of the alpha of the werewolves and Tilda was a witch. Centuries of animosity between witches and werewolves meant that the idea of the probable next alpha committing himself to a witch was an impossible thought. Tilda saw that, so she had been blindsided by his confession. Add to that the fact that until twenty-four hours ago she had been in love with somebody else, you could say that Eamon confessing his long-suppressed feelings for her was causing a bit of an uncomfortable situation. Not helped by the dwarf who enjoyed life most when he was messing with somebody. There was no way that Pike was going to give up his seat next to Tilda without violence being involved. Since Pike

9

was obviously not going to be as amenable as Karl had been, Eamon dropped down in the seat next to the dwarf, the vicious glare on his face promising retribution. I looked down the row. This covered almost everybody in town who knew I was a cursebreaker. I raised my head when I heard the sound of hooves and couldn't help the smile that crossed my face when I saw Dr Collias standing at the end of our row. He may not be able to sit due to the fact he was a centaur, but I knew he was making a statement. Although he didn't technically know I was a cursebreaker, he was pretty sure he'd worked it out.

For the first time since I'd been forced to expose my ability to my friends to save Tilda's life, the terror that had gripped me began to recede. These people were willing to stand by my side. I had no reason to doubt that there would be others. Sure, like Tilda said, there would be the rabid few who wanted my head, but maybe that wouldn't be as bad as I thought it was going to be.

The noise in the crowd rose and I looked up to see the Town Council was entering the hall. As usual, Aidan Tolan came in first. There was no way the werewolf would ever let himself come second to anybody. As Conall's and Eamon's father, you would think I would have at least a civil relationship with him. You would be wrong. Flora came into the hall behind Aidan. Usually, she had a serene expression on her face. Today was different. She looked haggard, as if she was weighed down by responsibility. I did that to her. My existence had taken away that peace from her. I hated that. Behind Flora came Aliana, the leader of the nymphs. I couldn't help but be envious of the graceful way she carried herself. She also inspired some concern. I knew from previous meetings that Aliana Pantelis was strict when it came to laws. I didn't see her bending those views for me. Next came Cary Heavyfoot of the dwarf clan, followed by

Dorota Bisek of the giants. Those two were as opposite in size as you would find, but the times I'd seen them, they had both been fair and willing to approach difficult situations in a pragmatic way. I hoped that held true today.

As the five councilors made their way to the front of the meeting hall and took their seats, I felt Conall squeeze my hand. He leaned over and whispered in my ear. "You're safe. I won't let anything happen to you."

I gave him a small smile and squeezed back. I wished I believed him, but I had a bad feeling that not even a berserker could protect me from the train wreck that was heading in my direction.

efore the meeting started, the door at the back of the hall opened and slammed shut. All eyes turned and my heart sank as the two magisters who were left in town entered. I knew that it had been a long shot, but I had hoped that there would be at least five minutes between the time my role as a cursebreaker was announced to the entire town, and the time when the people who had the ability to arrest me found out. It looked like I wasn't that lucky. I couldn't help myself watching as Julian Bernauer and Penelope Hartford found seats close to the Path coven. I glanced at Conall and was concerned to see an expression of anger on his face.

I watched as Flora stood up and took her place at the podium. The crowd instantly went silent and Flora gave a tight smile.

"Recently, we have had a tumultuous time in Walker Bay. Three months ago, I was cursed by Isobel Fulton who wanted to assume power of the Walker Bay Coven. That curse was broken. Since then there have been many curses cast in Walker Bay, most notably the plague which hit our town, targeting the first-born sons."

A murmuring started in the room. There had to have been some people who suspected curses were causing the problems in the town, but for the last few hundred years, curses had been such a rarity that it would not have even crossed their mind as an option. I knew that there had been many theories of how the plague started, including an idea that Walker Bay had been experimented on by the military. It seemed outlandish conspiracy theories were also a favorite pastime of the paranormal.

I glanced over at Aidan Tolan, knowing that if I wanted to gauge how the worst of Walker Bay was going to react to this news, he would be my litmus test. From the anger showing in his expression, things weren't going well.

"I have reason to believe that Walker Bay has been targeted and that there are many other curses that have been seeded throughout the town, just waiting to go off."

That quiet murmuring was rising as people started to understand what Flora was saying.

"How did this happen? What have you done?"

I should have expected Violet Hallybread to be the first to undermine Flora. As one of the three leaders of the Path coven, she was always looking for ways to blame Flora and to push her agenda. "Has the Walker Bay coven been dabbling in forbidden magic?"

Flora swung her attention to the woman who had been a thorn in her side for years. "Unfortunately, it was Ilsa Hocking who created the curse that caused the plague."

"That's not possible," spluttered Violet and the rest of the Path coven were muttering angrily behind her.

When we first made the decision to announce what I was, I had wondered how much of the truth Flora was going to tell, and how much she was going to conceal for the sake of town unity. It seemed that Flora had made the decision to lay it all out.

"She was angry that her daughter had been murdered and lashed out at those she felt were responsible. She also wanted to make the entire town suffer the way she was suffering."

Most people would have stopped at the revelation that their co-leader had broken one of their most sacred rules. Violet Hallybread was not most people.

"That is a vicious lie." Violet glanced quickly at Julian Bernauer. I was pretty sure that she wouldn't want her magister son to have heard that. "Nobody in the Path coven would ever dabble in dark magic."

I winced as I knew where Flora would go next.

"Jeanette Hocking was also using curses to hide her affairs."

My eyes instantly swung to Aidan and I could see the way he tensed. Very few people knew that he had been having an affair with Jeanette Hocking. Even less knew that she had also been having an affair with his son, Brian, who had been the one to kill her to break the hold she had over him and his father. A hold that was magical in nature. Mostly.

Instead of refuting the charge like I expected her to, Violet sat down, the fight seeming to have gone out of her. My eyes widened as the realization washed over me that Violet knew what Jeanette had been doing. She might not have known about the curse, but she'd known about Jeanette's affairs. I glanced at Flora and saw that she had come to the same conclusion.

"In the last week we have found that common household items have been cursed and at least one of those curses may have been cast decades ago. These curses are now being triggered in a random manner." Her eyes swept the crowd who looked stunned by her revelations. "If you have purchased anything from a Traveler witch, you need to bring it to the coven library so it can be evaluated to determine if it has been cursed. If you are struck down by lesions or burns you need to go to the clinic immediately so it can be determined if you have been affected by one of these curses."

An elderly woman struggled to her feet. I vaguely remembered seeing her at the Walker Bay coven meetings. Hopefully that meant she'd go a bit easier on the coven leader. Although Flora did encourage her members to not be afraid to speak up, so this could go either way.

"Why is this happening?"

Flora gave a resigned smile. "Because we exist. No other town has this many races living in relative peace with each other. We embody the future when so many are stuck in the past. I'm not saying we're a perfect example of a community. We are far from it, but at least we try to live together peacefully."

"Is this an internal failing of the witch covens?"

I winced at the pointed question from Dorota Bisek. It seemed the councilors were not willing to just sit back and accept what Flora was saying.

Flora looked over at the giant, a regretful expression on her face. "Despite the Conclave's best efforts, we have always known that curses were not completely stamped out. The fact we have had such a strong resurgence is a matter of great concern. Although I would say that this is not an overall problem, I do feel that Walker Bay has been targeted by one or more very powerful witches, and they are using others to create chaos in our community. These witches may not even be associated with Walker Bay. As I've said, we have reason to believe that a Traveler witch is behind some of the curses we have seen so far."

"What can we do?" The lyrical voice of Aliana Pantelis cut through the hall and, despite her calm tone, I could tell she was worried. "My understanding is that curses cannot be broken. What good will it do us to discover these curses if there is nothing we can do about them."

Flora took in a deep breath and I could tell from the way her eyes sought mine that she was about to announce my secret.

"That is correct," Flora agreed. "It is usually impossible for a curse to be broken once it is cast."

"I thought the Walker Bay coven broke the curse that Isobel Fulton cast on you or was there something else involved." The dwarf representative had a shrewd expression on his face as he interrupted Flora.

I glanced over at Pike, wondering how much his clan leader knew. He shrugged in my direction. Whatever suspicions Cary Heavyfoot might have, it looked like he hadn't shared them with the deputy.

Flora looked towards the dwarf leader and I was surprised at the smile on her face. "You're partly right. My coven, despite their best efforts were unable to break the curse. They were never going to be able to break it."

"And yet you are standing here," drawled Dorota, her keen eyes curious.

"Yes," Flora said, and she straightened as she turned her head and looked directly at me. "I'm alive because of a curse-breaker."

She would have said more but she was drowned out by the rising volume as the crowd realized what she was saying. I looked closely and could see that the majority of those that had taken to their feet and were yelling questions at the front of the room were from the Path coven. Members of the Walker Bay coven seemed to be glued to their seats, stunned expressions on their faces. Until this moment they had been sure that they had been the ones to save their leader. To learn that they hadn't and that she had been allowing them to believe that they had broken the curse was surely going to have repercussions.

"Silence!" Dorota Bisek bellowed and I was sure that the walls of the building shook.

It took a couple of minutes for the room to be brought under control again. Before Flora could begin talking a strong voice rang out.

"That's an interesting claim considering the last of the cursebreakers died out three hundred years ago."

I wasn't surprised that Julian had decided to tackle this situation head on.

"You mean they were wiped out, don't you?" Flora replied.

Julian inclined his head. "Regardless, cursebreakers do not exist."

I could tell from the movement in her shoulders that Flora was gathering strength. "I beg to differ. My niece, Sadie, is a cursebreaker. Over the last few months she has protected this town from whoever is attacking it by destroying the curses." Flora swept her eyes across the room as if catching the gaze of every single person. "That includes the plague that recently tore through this town. It wasn't me who saved the lives of the firstborn sons who were struck down by Ilsa Hocking's curse. It was Sadie. Without her we would have lost a significant number of men from this town, including you, Magister Bernauer."

I could see Julian wanted to say more but he was stunned by Flora's revelation. Unfortunately, his mother wasn't as afflicted, and she jumped to her feet.

"Cursebreakers are evil. There was a reason they were wiped out."

The expression on Violet Hallybread's face was apoplectic. I could see that Flora was struggling to hold back her anger at the other coven leader's desperate need to score points.

"Cursebreakers were wiped out because the Conclave was afraid of the power behind them and gave no thought to the person. My niece has proved time and again that she is only concerned with protecting the people in Walker Bay. At no time has she shown any interest in learning how to cast curses herself."

"Why exactly have you decided to call a town meeting to announce this?" drawled Cary Heavyfoot. "I would have thought that this was the kind of thing you'd keep quiet."

Flora nodded. "That was our original plan," she sighed. "Unfortunately, something has happened to tip our hand. Recently there have been several curses that have targeted random members of the community. We have reason to believe that those curses were triggered for the sole purpose of finding the cursebreaker in town. We were concerned that this pattern would continue until whoever was doing it had a definitive answer. By announcing that Sadie is the cursebreaker, we are hoping to stop innocent people from getting hurt."

"You're taking a huge risk," Dorota commented.

"I know," Flora replied. "We just couldn't see any other options."

While this was all going on, I could hear the whispers happening around me. I stared straight ahead, watching the Council members as they discussed what Flora's announcement might mean for the town.

Conall squeezed my hand and leaned over to kiss me on the cheek. I knew he meant for it to be a sign of his support to all the people who were watching us. I smiled at him, grateful for his strength. There was a part of me that was horrified by what we were doing. I just didn't see any other choice. I drew in a shaky breath. It was too late to second guess my decision now, and make no mistake, it had been my decision.

I noticed that the murmuring had become louder as the Council members had taken to talking amongst themselves. This stopped when Dorota brought her fist down on the table in front of her. The sound reverberated through the hall and the noise stopped.

"Thank you, Flora, for informing us of an issue that is facing Walker Bay." She straightened and looked directly at the crowd. "Sadie Goodwin has performed a service for this town, and she is willing to continue to provide that service. I would suggest we focus on the here and now and leave ancient superstitions and mistakes where they belong."

She hit the table again and the meeting ended. I watched as the Council members started to leave the stage and make their way to the back of the hall. As they walked past the row of seats where I was sitting, Dorota Bisek stopped.

"You have my support." She turned toward me, and I could see an expression of gratitude on her face. "My son was one of those you saved. I can never repay you for what you did for him and for all the others in my clan." She drew in a shaky breath as the memory of those days when we weren't sure what was happening with the men in the town washed over her. "If you need sanctuary, come to us. We will protect you."

"Thank you," I replied, feeling a little teary myself. Tilda had told me that people had noticed my actions during the plague. Seems she was right.

Most of the Council members had been waylaid by members of their clans and I could see that Flora was in the middle of a group that weren't going to let her go. I had a feeling both covens were going to want exhaustive explanations regarding what having a cursebreaker in town meant for them. I was surprised that the werewolves seemed to be making a break for it. That was very unlike them. Since I'd come to Walker Bay, I'd found the werewolves were pretty consistent in their willingness to tackle any situation head on, especially when it came to witches. I would have thought they would have had more to say

I was distracted by the sheriff talking to Karl in a low voice and then standing up as if to leave.

"Where are you going?" I hated the note of panic in my voice. Despite the fact that I was surrounded by people who had made a public statement by standing by my side, I knew that the sheriff was the only one who really made me feel safe.

Conall's eyes softened and he pulled me up and wrapped his arms around me. "You're going to be safe," he murmured against my ear. "I'm just making sure that the magisters are aware of what the consequences will be if they choose to exercise a Conclave precept at this point in time. Walker Bay is not a Conclave town. Our laws come first, and that includes protecting our citizens from outdated genocidal beliefs."

"Okay," I nodded. "Just don't let Julian bait you into anything. He can be really irritating when he wants to be."

Conall barked out a sharp laugh. "Thanks for the tip, but I'd already worked that out."

With another quick squeeze, he let go and made his way down the row before heading for the magisters who were in the middle of an animated discussion with the Path coven. From the expressions on their faces, it didn't look like the sheriff's interruption was welcome.

The entire time Conall was talking to them, Julian kept his eyes trained on me. I wish I knew what was going through his head. Until an hour ago Julian had repeatedly professed to coming back to Walker Bay for the sole reason of convincing me to break up with Conall and find my happily ever after with him. I had a feeling I had added yet another wrinkle to his plans. I sighed as I realized that in a way this solved one of my problems. The only reason for Julian to come near me now was to arrest me and drag me back to the Conclave. It looked like something good had come out of this decision.

Tilda put a hand on my arm. "Do you want to get going?"

I nodded. I was beginning to feel claustrophobic as every set of eyes seemed to be on me. There wasn't much I could do about my cursebreaker abilities. I only hoped now that the news was out, I could go about my life without all the secrecy and fear. It was probably an unrealistic hope, but I was holding onto it.

As we made our way through the crowd, I couldn't help but smile at the way my friends had spaced themselves around me, as if giving me the maximum amount of protection. Just before we got to the doorway, I was surprised to see Tilda's grandmother making her way out of the hall. I would have expected her to stay close to Flora or at least to start peppering me with questions. As the person who kidnapped me and brought me to this town, she was in part responsible for this situation. I tapped her on the shoulder and was surprised when she started to back away from me.

"I'm sorry, I've got somewhere I have to be. I don't have time…" She rushed off.

"I wonder what's wrong with her," Tilda commented.

I didn't reply because I knew what was wrong with her. In the moment before she rushed off, I saw something in Maude's eyes that I never expected to see. I saw fear.

4

J wasn't entirely sure why I'd let Tilda talk me into going to the diner to grab something to eat. You would have thought that the correct course of action after dropping a bomb like we had on the town, would have been to stay out of sight and let everybody calm down before continuing on with my life as if nothing had happened. It seemed Tilda felt differently and, considering I hadn't eaten all day because of nerves, it didn't take much to convince me it was a good idea.

Usually when I'd come into the diner I was greeted with an underlying sense of hostility. Between the women who were unhappy that I was the Destined Beloved of the sheriff, and the werewolves who blamed me for the incarceration of one of the alpha's sons, I'd managed to make myself pretty unpopular with a certain subset of the population in a short period of time. Today was different. It seemed everybody was giving me as much space as possible which I felt was a little unfair. It wasn't like I had started sacrificing babies or done anything else that warranted the fearful reaction I was getting. It also wasn't like I was the first person in town to drop the news that I was a member of a group that hadn't been alive for hundreds of years. The sheriff had announced he was a berserker and people had seemed to accept it. Except for the werewolves who tossed him out of the clan. Maybe it wasn't so well-received. At least the witches hadn't thrown me out of the coven. Of course, it had only been a little over forty minutes since the announcement. I'm sure being disowned probably took a little time.

"Do you know what worries me the most?" I asked as I checked to make sure my privacy spell was activated.

"You've narrowed it down to one thing?"

I grinned at the sarcasm in her remark. I could see that Tilda was a little annoyed at people's reaction to me. "Why didn't Aidan start screaming for my head?"

Tilda paused as she started thinking. "Huh, you're right. That was weird."

If there was anybody in this town who should have relished the opportunity to stick the boot in, it would have been the alpha of the werewolf clan. Add to that the information that there were rogue witches casting curses on the town, Aidan Tolan should have been in his element calling for my banishment to the Glen with the rest of the outcasts, and for Flora to be stood down as coven leader and member of the Town Council.

"It's not good, is it?"

Tilda nodded gravely. "At least when Aidan is yelling, you know where you stand. Him keeping his mouth shut is a really bad sign."

"Sadie, can I talk to you?"

My mouth went dry as I looked up into the eyes of my ex-boyfriend. I honestly didn't know how to reply.

"I'm not sure that's a good idea." Seeing my inability to

think up a good reason to avoid this situation, Tilda decided to step in.

Julian's eyes did not waver. "I really think it would be a good idea for us to talk. I think you owe me that."

And that was enough to break me out of my stunned silence. "Owe you? I don't owe you a thing." I could not believe his gall.

Julian didn't even have the sense to look a little shamefaced at his claim. He just stood there with an expectant expression.

"Fine, let's get this over and done with," I gritted out.

Tilda raised an eyebrow.

"It'll be fine," I reassured her as I stood up. "I'm not going anywhere with him. You can keep a close eye on us the entire time."

I slid into the empty booth opposite us and indicated for Julian to join me. I clasped my hands in front of me and raised my chin as I prepared myself for what was to come.

"Why didn't you tell me?"

It looked like we were starting with the stupid questions.

"You're asking me why I didn't come to a magister with the fact that I was a cursebreaker who you have a legal obligation to drag to the Conclave to be executed? I've heard the stories about what the magisters did to the cursebreaker families. I wasn't really willing to test you."

Julian reached out and placed his hand on top of mine. "I would never have done that to you."

I pulled my hands out from underneath his. "I don't know that. I barely know you, Julian. You lied to me the entire time we were together and then you left me without any warning, only to turn up in this town breathing fire about rogue witches." I waved my hand in the direction of my friend. "Tilda only found out yesterday. Nobody knew."

"How about the sheriff?"

I pulled up short at his question. "Well, yes, Conall knew."

"Of course, he did," muttered Julian, his tone showing how annoyed he was by my response.

I leaned back in my seat. "What do you want from me, Julian? I didn't ask for this ability, but I can't say that I wish I didn't have it. I've been able to help too many people for me to do that. We're just not keeping it a secret anymore."

"Why is that?" Julian asked shrewdly. "I mean, why announce something like this? You had to know that it would bring the attention of the Conclave."

I paused as I tried to think of the best answer I could give him. I didn't want to tell him that one of his team had been so determined to find the cursebreaker in Walker Bay that he had been triggering old curses all over town, but it looked like I didn't have a choice. The Conclave had been given the barest of details about what had happened with Liam Rigby. I knew that Julian had been desperately trying to discover the truth, but the Conclave had told him to stand down and accept that Liam had transgressed the laws of Walker Bay and would need to pay for it.

"Liam knew there was a cursebreaker in town. The curses that have been happening were his way of testing to discover who it was."

Julian shook his head. "No, that's not possible."

I looked worriedly over at Tilda, glad that she couldn't hear this conversation.

"We found out when he put a curse on Tilda purely to force me to use my ability in a public setting. He wanted irrefutable proof of what I was. I won't allow the people I care about to be used in that way." I stood up and slid out of the booth. "If the Conclave wants their cursebreaker, tell them to come after me, not my friends."

Julian caught my hand as I indicated to Tilda that I was ready to leave.

"I still care about you. This doesn't change anything."

I looked down at our joined hands and swallowed as I raised my eyes to his. "It changes everything."

5

I woke up slowly and, for a brief couple of seconds, I forgot what we had done and the possible consequences I could be facing. All too soon the memories of the previous day came flooding back and I sighed as I got up and started getting ready for my day. After leaving the diner with Tilda I had retreated to my home and continued my unending job of making the place livable. Now that the curse that had inhabited the place for years had been broken, it felt like the house had been given a new lease on life and I intended to make it my sanctuary. After the last few months, I had a feeling I was going to need it. I had worked until exhaustion had overtaken me and dropped off as soon as my head hit the pillow. I figured I must have slept like the dead, because that is the only reason I could think of to explain how I missed something very important that became obvious when I went downstairs.

"What are you doing here?"

Conall stretched his arms above his head and yawned as he peered up at me from my couch. "I'm protecting my Destined Beloved. What does it look like I'm doing?"

"It looks like you came into my house without my express permission, Sheriff," I said, the annoyance obvious in my tone. "You really should stop doing that."

Conall sat up and squinted as he realized I might not be as enamored at what he'd done as he thought I would be.

"We don't know how the Conclave is going to react to your announcement. Before long, this news is going to filter through to the rest of the paranormal world. Everybody will be watching."

I was confused. "Wasn't that the idea? Make sure that the Conclave knew they couldn't spirit me away in the darkness?"

Conall gave me a grim smile. "That's what we're hoping for. I just don't trust them not to come at you another way. Until we know how they are going to react, I would prefer you not take any chances with your safety. Always make sure that you are with other people and I intend to be here every night."

"I'm not really sure how I'm feeling about this." I waved my hand between the two of us.

Conall sighed. "You know we would have been past this if I hadn't…"

"Had a brain snap and run off?" I said sweetly.

I could see that Conall was trying very hard not to get annoyed with me. It was really unfortunate for him that, for once, I wasn't the one to blame for this situation.

With a heavy sigh he pulled himself to his feet and I worked very hard not to stare at his bare chest. "I messed up. I let my numerous issues from the way I was raised to cloud what we have. I can't promise that I won't do something stupid again, but I can promise that I'll be better at communicating my stupidity."

"That's all I ask," I said as I turned and headed for the kitchen. "Did you want some breakfast? I can't guarantee the quality as cooking has never been one of my skills, but it should be edible."

"No thanks, I'll pick something up after I drop you off at Arthur McClune's place."

That's right. Since arriving in Walker Bay, it had been discovered that despite my curse breaking power, the rest of my magical abilities were woefully inadequate. I had managed to successfully craft the grand total of one spell, that being the plastic troll doll with a privacy spell attached to it. A feat that to most witches was considered somewhat pathetic. For some reason I just didn't get it. After several fruitless weeks of trying to help me get at least a basic understanding, Flora had passed me along to Arthur McClune in the hope that learning the historical basis for witchcraft would help me find the magic inside. I wouldn't say that it had been a raging success, but Flora was insistent, and I was retaining some of the information, despite his impression of the most boring history teacher you could possibly imagine.

"Yay," I said tonelessly. "Exciting day for me."

Conall grinned as he headed up the stairs. "I'm just going to grab a quick shower. I'll be ready soon."

I busied myself downstairs as I concentrated on not picturing the sheriff naked in my bathroom. I was grateful for the distraction when somebody knocked on my front door. Expecting Tilda, I didn't check before I opened the door. That may have been a mistake.

"What are you doing here?" I groaned at the sight of Julian at my front doorstep first thing in the morning.

"We need to talk," he replied. "Can I come in?"

"I really think that's a bad idea," I said urgently, knowing that with Conall's werewolf hearing, he already knew that I had an ex-boyfriend standing on my porch wanting to come inside. Sure enough, I could already hear the heavy tread of his footsteps as he came downstairs at a faster pace than he went up them.

"What are you doing here, Bernauer?" he growled as he stepped beside me, his hair wet and his shirt not yet buttoned up. I had a feeling that was not an oversight.

Julian's face flushed with anger and it didn't take a genius to work out what he was imagining. It didn't help when Conall put an arm around me and raised an eyebrow.

"I need to talk to you, Sadie," Julian replied, refusing to look at the sheriff.

"Anything you have to say to Sadie goes through me."

Whatever response Conall was expecting, I'm pretty sure that Julian laughing at him wasn't it. "I don't know why you worry me. If you truly believe that, you don't know her at all." He grinned at me. "Now, will you talk to me?"

"I thought we covered everything last night," I said, deciding to shrug off Conall's attempt to control this situation. Julian was right. The sheriff should know better by now.

"The Conclave wants to see you."

Despite knowing that this was an inevitable result of our actions the night before, just hearing Julian say those words was enough to make my throat clench. This was it.

"The Conclave will convene a special session so you can plead your case and I will accompany you to speak on your behalf."

He looked so earnest as if this was the best thing that could happen. I hated to burst his bubble.

"I am not going to be taken in front of the Conclave by a magister. I haven't committed any crime and I refuse to be judged based on something I have no control over." I shook my head as Julian tried to interrupt. "I was born this way. I don't recognize an organization that believes I should be put to death based on a law that should never have been instituted in the first place."

I could feel myself shaking at the thought of what he was proposing. Conall gave me a squeeze as if to confirm that I didn't have to deal with this alone.

Julian shook his head. "I would never allow them to hurt you," he swore.

"I know that," I said, feeling a surge of compassion for the man I once believed I loved. "The problem is, you might not be given the choice."

I could see that Julian wanted to argue but one look at me told him everything he needed to know. I wasn't moving on this. There was no way that I was going to be taken to see the Conclave. If they wanted me, they were going to have to come and get me.

Julian straightened his shoulders and nodded. "Very well. I will inform the Conclave that you refuse to attend the session."

Conall stepped forward as Julian went to walk away. "You should also inform the Conclave that the Assembly is taking an interest in this situation. They have offered sanctuary to Sadie if the Conclave chooses to take action against her. They also condemn in the harshest possible terms any attempts to return to the old ways. They will be watching."

↑

*a*fter Julian left us, Conall and I got in his truck and headed for Arthur McClune's house.

After a few moments of silence, I turned to him. "Was that true, what you said about the Assembly?"

Conall nodded. "I spent last night speaking to representatives of a lot of the paranormal races and there was a consensus. If the witches start thinking that it is acceptable to restart a genocide in the twenty-first century, then we have bigger problems than we thought. That would be a clear indication that the Conclave believes their law holds dominion over all other laws. That is not something that can be allowed to stand."

I knew the Assembly was the governing body for all paranormal races and the Conclave set the laws for witches. In my mind it would be problematic for two legal systems to be working side by side, but I'd been assured it worked. I had a feeling this situation was going to test that system.

As we pulled up on McClune's property I couldn't help the sigh that came out of me. My life used to be simple. Since coming to Walker Bay, it had become significantly more difficult.

After he parked the truck, Conall turned to me and cupped my face with his hand. "Everything's going to be okay," he said, his thumb stroking my cheek.

"It's not that," I assured him. "I'm just wondering why it has to be so complicated. Despite what certain people believe, I'm not interested in global domination or resurrecting the witches as the strongest of the paranormals. I just want to live a quiet life with the people I've found here. Except for the curse breaking ability, I'm really not much of a witch."

"I beg to differ," Conall murmured as his head dropped towards me.

I didn't get a chance to stop him and if I was perfectly honest, I didn't want to. I'd missed this feeling as his lips molded to mine, the certainty that nothing else mattered except the man who had me gathered in his arms. Conall was kissing me like he'd just come out of prison and in a way he had. Our relationship had been weird lately and we'd lost our faith in the inevitability of the Destined Beloved prophecy.

I wasn't given much of a chance to enjoy the feelings he was evoking because, like so many before us, we were disturbed by an angry old man knocking on the window.

Conall's head jerked up and I could see from the look in his eyes that he was not happy to be interrupted.

"What?" he snarled as the window went down.

"You're making out on my property, son. You don't really have the right to be angry."

Despite his supposed annoyance, I could see that McClune was enjoying having the upper hand with the sheriff. I grinned as Conall deliberately put the window back up.

"Is he always this irritating?" It didn't take a genius to tell that Conall was a little frustrated that we were interrupted. Considering this was the closest we'd come to recapturing the easy affection we'd had before he'd taken off, I had a feeling McClune had just made himself very unpopular. Not that anybody was particularly fond of him to begin with.

I laughed as I opened the door. "You might want to remember this moment next time you're busting a couple of teenagers steaming up a car. Maybe have a little compassion."

The sheriff grunted, but I could see the smile curving his lips. I closed the door and waved as he drove off.

I turned around to find that McClune had already headed off in the direction of the river that flowed close to his house. With a resigned air I followed him. When we reached the clearing, I was not surprised that he stood silently, staring at the river, his back towards me.

"What are you doing here?" he barked suddenly.

I would have thought it was obvious. "I believe you're supposed to teach me about magic."

"I doubt there's much I can teach a cursebreaker."

I grimaced. "You've heard."

For the first time the elderly witch turned to face me. "Cursebreakers are considered the most powerful of witches. You don't need my help. My understanding is you've already managed to tap into your power."

"Yeah, about that." I sat down on the ground and crossed my legs. "I'm going to need all the information on curse-breakers that you've got, because I've got a feeling I'm not quite as powerful as everybody thinks."

I could see McClune's frown and I decided I may as well tell him everything. "I managed to punch through a shield that Liam Rigby had erected around himself, and I almost destroyed him. I did destroy a bunch of trees." I frowned at the memory. "I feel really bad about the trees."

McClune studied me. "Breaking through a magister's

shield is a pretty significant thing to do. If you don't think that's power, you're not paying attention."

"The problem is, I'm not sure it was my power that I used."

For the first time since I met him, it looked like I'd said something that Arthur McClune found interesting. "What do you mean?"

I paused as I tried to work out the best way to explain this. "Since I arrived in Walker Bay, I've been dealing with curses. I think that each time I break a curse, I absorb something from it. I'm not sure if it's power or knowledge, or what it is. I just think that a part of every curse I break is lodging inside me. That was what I used to punch through that shield. That power wasn't mine. It came from whoever has been laying these curses around Walker Bay."

I waited for a response to my revelation until the silence became unbearable.

"Well, what do you think?"

McClune shrugged. "I think that regardless of where the power is coming from, the fact you can wield it makes you dangerous." He looked up at the sky as if trying to find a nice way to say something. "Did you notice anything else about yourself in the days preceding the incident?"

I frowned as I tried to remember. "I was really emotional. My moods kept swinging between sad and angry. I got irritated easily and I may have overreacted a bit to some relationship issues."

"Could it have been...?"

I pointed a finger at the elderly witch. "You even think of saying hormones, and you're going to find out on a personal level what happened to those trees."

McClune cleared his throat, a look of discomfort on his face. "You could be right. The curses you're breaking may be having an effect on your personality. It would certainly

35

explain why so many cursebreakers have fallen so spectacularly to the darkness."

That did not sound good. "You need to tell me how to stop that from happening."

McClune barked out a rusty laugh. "What makes you think I have that kind of information?"

I threw my hands up in the air. "You're the one who's supposed to know everything. At least that's what Flora thinks. I need someone to tell me what I can do and how to control it."

McClune watched me keenly. "First suggestion I'd make would be to stop having anything to do with curses. If what you are saying is correct and you're absorbing some of the curse every time you break them, you're going to want to stop doing that."

"That's brilliant," I said, sarcasm dripping from every word. "I'll just get on that, and the next time some crazy witch decides to send out a plague to kill all the firstborn sons, I'll just let it go because my bad mood is more important than their lives."

McClune lowered himself to the ground across from me. "You're still feeling the emotional upset, aren't you?"

I nodded. "A little. Not as much as I was before the confrontation with Liam Rigby, but I'm still a little unsettled."

"Very well," he replied. "I want you to lie back, close your eyes, and tell me everything that has happened from the moment you came to Walker Bay. I don't want you to leave out anything. If we are going to get control of this, I need to know the complete truth. No holding back."

After a moment I lay down on the ground, closed my eyes and started talking. I went through every moment since the day Maude Atwill and Margot Fulton kidnapped me in the hope that I could save their coven leader.

When I finished, several hours later, my throat felt dry and my head hurt. I looked over at the elderly man and found him staring at me intently as if he was trying to peer into my soul.

"Is that everything?" he asked.

I pulled myself up into a sitting position and reached into my bag for a bottle of water, enjoying the sweet relief as the water flowed down my throat.

"That's everything," I croaked, "minus a few of the more personal things that have happened, but you really don't need to know those."

McClune's eyes gleamed. "After what I saw in the sheriff's truck, I'm pretty sure I can fill in the rest."

For my own peace of mind, I was going to ignore the fact he had just said that. I waited impatiently for him to dazzle me with his brilliant insights.

"So, what do you think?"

McClune turned towards me and I could see tension in his face. "I don't think the person doing this is a cursebreaker," he said.

I hadn't even thought of that as a possibility, but now I could see that was a real fear for him. "Then what are they?"

McClune looked up at the sky as if searching for answers. "I think you have a rogue witch who specializes in dark magic. The fact they can slip into Walker Bay without anyone being the wiser tells me that they are a powerful technical witch. I'm not discounting that they have some natural talent. What I'm saying is that they have a lot of knowledge, and they are using that knowledge to cause a lot of issues, but it hasn't tipped over into true cursebreaker territory. Cursebreakers aren't just stronger witches. They are in a completely different league." He paused as if searching for an example. "Wars, pestilence, famine. Those are the hallmarks of a cursebreaker. Where's the challenge in making a football team of teenage boys a little extra aggressive when you've got the ability to virtually wipe out an entire generation of young men through war? The plague that was unleashed by Ilsa Hocking was limited to just the town of Walker Bay and it didn't hit every firstborn, only a percentage of them. A cursebreaker could unleash a plague that wipes out an entire continent."

I felt sick. I didn't blame Maude for looking at me with fear at the meeting. Frankly, if I had a mirror, I was pretty sure that I would find that I had the same expression on my face now.

It looked like McClune noticed my horrified expression as well, because, for once, his expression softened. "I'm not saying that is going to happen to you. I'm saying you are going to have to fight to ensure that is not your future, especially if whoever is doing this is infecting you with their evil every time you break one of their curses." He pulled himself to his feet. "I'm going to pull together some information and we'll talk more tomorrow. Not every cursebreaker went bad. There must be a way for you to resist the dark magic."

I stood up and grabbed my bag. "I think that's a good idea. If I'm going to deal with this, I need as much information as possible." I lowered my voice, despite the fact we were alone and I was pretty sure the clearing was warded against casual listeners. "I'd also like you to look into whether it is possible to bind a cursebreaker's powers."

From the way McClune's eyes widened I could see that I had managed to shock him. "You would allow yourself to be bound?"

"If it's a choice between that and becoming what everybody is fearing, then I don't see that I have many options."

At some time in the last two days I had made that decision. The power I had felt coursing through me when I was angry at Liam Rigby for hurting my friend frightened me.

The thought that I would come to enjoy using that power terrified me.

"I'll be back tomorrow," I said as I started walking out of the clearing. "We'll talk more about my options then."

I felt a hand on my arm, and I turned slightly and stumbled as I felt something slam into me. I looked down and was shocked to see an arrow sticking out of my chest. For an instant I didn't feel anything, but then I must have moved because pain streaked through me.

I sagged against McClune and was surprised at the strength in the old man as he managed to keep a hold on me while lowering me to the ground. I saw him looking around frantically as if desperate to find where the attack was coming from. He curled his hand around where the large arrow entered my body and pressed down. I screamed. I knew he was trying to stop the bleeding but the pain was indescribable. With my final bit of strength, I pushed against him, desperate to make him stop but he refused to let go. Weakness stole through me and my arms dropped. Despite my best efforts, I could feel myself drifting away and the last thing I saw was the horrified expression on Arthur McClune's face as he implored me to stay with him.

7

I blinked at the lights above me. My brain told me they were dim but as I opened my eyes, I felt like I was staring into the sun. I slammed them shut again and squinted as I tried to get my eyes to adjust.

"That's it, Sadie. Open your eyes for me."

I started at the sound of a voice close by and moved my head, crying out as pain coursed through me.

"No, don't move," Conall murmured beside me, his voice sounding hoarse. "Just open your beautiful eyes. Let me see them. Please."

I tried again and only felt a small amount of burning as I opened them fully.

"That's right," Conall soothed. "You're going to be okay."

Now that my eyes were open, I could see that I was in the town clinic, and Conall was lying on the bed next to me.

"Are you allowed to be here?" I croaked. I was pretty sure the doctor would have an opinion on visitors who shared the beds of unconscious patients.

Conall gently pushed himself up and I frowned when I saw his haggard appearance. "I got special permission. I figured if you got so upset at me sneaking into your house and sleeping on your couch, you'd be apoplectic at me being in your bed without your express invitation. I was hoping you'd wake up and yell at me."

There was something in the way that he said that. "How long?"

"Five days." Conall's voice broke and I could see him wiping at his eyes. "You were shot five days ago."

"Who?"

A grim expression settled on the sheriff's face. "We're working on that."

The door opened and I heard the clattering of hooves. "Seems you were right, Sheriff. She doesn't like it when you get in her bed without permission."

Conall smiled and brushed his lips against my cheek before moving as gently as he could and getting off the bed. I figured he'd move back and give the doctor some space to carry out an examination, but he stayed by my bedside and grasped my hand as if refusing to let go.

Dr Collias smiled as he looked down at me. "Well, young lady, you gave us quite the scare."

I licked my dry lips. "Could I have some water, please?" I whispered.

"Of course."

The doctor used the controls to raise the bed until I was in a seated position and held the glass while I sipped through the straw. I could feel from the tension in Conall's hand that he was feeling the pain behind every whimper that I made.

"I'm okay," I whispered.

"No, you're not," he replied. "But you will be." He pulled up a chair beside the bed and sat down, bringing my hand to his lips and kissing it. "It was close," he croaked.

I squeezed his hand and faced the doctor. "How bad was it?"

"Do you remember what happened?" he asked.

I frowned as I tried to think. "I was shot by an arrow." I paled at the memory. "Why would somebody shoot me with an arrow?"

Dr Collias ignored my question. "The arrow entered your chest, just missing your heart. You were very fortunate."

I didn't feel particularly fortunate, but considering I was still here and conscious, I probably didn't have much room to complain. "How much damage?"

Collias pushed back his glasses which had started to slide down his nose. "Surprisingly, the damage isn't that extensive. You had a couple of fractured ribs, damaged tissue, but somehow it managed to avoid any major organs or arteries."

"That's good, isn't it?" I asked, concerned with the expression on his face.

Collias nodded. "Usually it would be." He drew in a deep breath. "The problem is that the arrowhead was coated in poison. That's what almost killed you. The fact you were only in a coma for five days is a miracle. We weren't sure if you would ever come out."

"Poison?" I croaked. "Somebody shot me with a poisoned arrow?"

Conall started stroking my hair as if he could wipe away my distress.

"What kind of poison was it?" I needed to know everything.

Collias glanced at Conall and he tightened the hold on my hand as if trying to will his strength into me.

"It was the venom from a three-headed serpent," Collias replied.

I had no idea what he was talking about.

Collias must have seen my confusion. "Three-headed serpents have always been considered creatures of myth, but they did exist, although I haven't heard of one being seen for centuries. Their poison is rare and always fatal."

I tried to process this. Somebody had tried to kill me. I could see that Collias and Conall were holding something back.

"What aren't you telling me?"

Conall sighed and I could tell he didn't want to answer. "The venom of the three-headed serpent on an arrow is the traditional method for killing a cursebreaker. It was the way the magisters were able to wipe them out."

And there it was. I hadn't expected such a quick and direct response from the Conclave. There went the hope that they had developed a sense of humanity in the last three hundred years.

"The Assembly has been notified and they have sent a protest to the Conclave," Conall continued. "The Conclave is insisting that they weren't behind the shooting."

Of course, they were.

I frowned as a panicked thought went through my mind. "Where's Flora?" I would have expected my aunt to be here. The fact that she wasn't meant something very bad had to have happened to her as well.

"She's fine," Conall soothed, guessing immediately where my thoughts had gone. "She and Tilda have been here the whole time. The doctor insisted they go home for the night. He said they were no good to you if they got too run down."

I glanced at Dr Collias. "Why didn't you tell Conall to go as well? He looks like he needs a decent sleep."

The doctor snorted. "I'm not that brave."

Considering he was the one person I knew willing to stand up to Flora who was the most powerful witch in Walker Bay, that statement said a lot.

I fought to get my thoughts into order. I needed to know more about what was happening, but my body was fighting against me. It was all too much and I was struggling to keep my eyes open.

"Don't go back to sleep." Conall's panicked voice cut through the fatigue.

Collias put his hand on the sheriff's shoulder. "She needs her rest. She's out of the coma but her body still needs to heal. Let her get some more sleep. The worst is over."

I felt my eyes drift shut as the doctor left the room. The bed dipped as Conall crawled in beside me and ever so gently put his arms around me. He rested his forehead against mine and I felt tears drop onto my cheeks.

"I can't lose you," he whispered and the pain in his voice sliced through me. "I've spent the last five days begging for you to wake up. This can never happen again."

I wanted to comfort him, but I couldn't make my body muster the energy to ease his pain.

"When you wake up, we are going to talk," Conall muttered. "I'm over this whole dancing around the prophecy thing. I know I've screwed up at times, but I love you and I am not risking losing you. I'm moving into your place and we are going to get married. You just need to accept that."

Trust Conall to come up with the worst proposal ever.

8

𝒴ou would think that my second attempt at waking up would be a peaceful one. I now knew what had happened and I knew that Conall was by my side, protecting me. My body was healing and I was in a medical clinic. I should have woken to the gentle ministrations of a nurse or at the very least a grumpy berserker werewolf still trying to convince me to marry him. Instead, I woke to the raised voices of two women just outside the doorway. I opened my eyes to find the sheriff torn between wanting to go and tell the women to shut up and not wanting to leave me.

"What's going on?" I asked as I smothered a yawn. I plucked at the hospital gown to have a look down my top, concerned by the weird smell emanating from the wound site. Medicine in Walker Bay consisted of a strange hybrid of modern medical knowledge and ancient witchcraft practices. Usually the result was quicker healing and better outcomes. Unfortunately, it also meant you had to deal with strange poultices on wounds which had a tendency to smell and feel a little funky. I wrinkled my nose and dropped the gown.

I was surprised at Conall's seeming reluctance to answer my question "What's happening out there?"

"A difference of opinion," he muttered as he helped me into a sitting position, growling at every hiss I made.

I frowned once I'd got comfortable. "That sounds like Flora. Who's she arguing with?"

Before he could answer the other voice rose above Flora's. "She is my granddaughter and I have every right to see her."

My startled eyes swung to Conall. "What the hell is going on?"

I could tell that the sheriff had hoped to put off this conversation, but considering how loud the argument outside my door was getting, I figured he had a maximum of five minutes before the situation degenerated to one he couldn't control without violence.

"Collette Harstone was informed about your shooting and she arrived two days ago. She is insisting that due to the fact that she is your grandmother, she has the right to make all medical decisions for you."

"How...why...what...?" I knew I wasn't making any sense, but this situation was leaving me dumbfounded. There was no way I wanted that woman determining what my medical options were. Considering the stories I'd heard about her, I wouldn't be surprised if she tried to yank the plug on me herself while the doctor wasn't looking.

Conall squeezed my hand. "Don't worry. As your Destined Beloved I have automatic control of all your medical care."

I really needed to learn more about the legal situation in paranormal towns. I had a feeling my lack of knowledge was going to come back and bite me in a big way at some stage.

"Nobody else needs to be making those decisions for me anymore. I am back on board. I'm going to be fine."

To illustrate my point, I flipped back the blankets, swung my legs over the other side of the bed and prepared to push myself to my feet.

Conall rushed around the bed to my side. "What do you think you're doing?" he growled.

"I need to go to the bathroom," I replied as I stood up and promptly sat back down again as the room started spinning.

"I'll take you."

He went to pick me up and I put a hand out to stop him.

"That is not going to happen. We are nowhere close to the point in our relationship where I am comfortable enough for you to accompany me to the bathroom. Get Flora or Tilda in here."

I could see Conall was annoyed, but I was not going to budge on this one. I still had some pride. He opened the door and I got my first glimpse of my grandmother. For some reason my initial reaction was relief that I looked nothing like her. She looked over and her eyes locked with mine. I refused to look away. I had a feeling that if I did, she would take it as a sign of weakness.

Conall's voice cut through the staring contest. "Sadie needs some help and she wants you, Flora."

From my position I could see Flora toss a triumphant look at Collette. I don't know why she was celebrating. Her victory in this competition meant she was taking me to the bathroom. I wouldn't exactly call that winning.

Flora slipped in and Conall closed the door very firmly in Collette's face. I was not even close to the point where I could think about what her being here meant to me.

My aunt came forward and very gently wrapped her arms around me. "I thought we'd lost you," she whispered and when she leaned back I could see the tears in her eyes.

"Cursebreaker, remember," I said, fighting my own tears. "Takes more than an arrow to the chest to take me down."

From the distressed looks my aunt and Destined Beloved threw to each other, I had a feeling that comment came a bit too soon.

"I just need some help getting to the bathroom," I mumbled.

"Of course," my aunt said.

Despite my objections, Conall scooped me up and walked me the few steps to the bathroom. At the door he gently lowered me to my feet and Flora quickly put an arm around my waist to support me. I tried very hard to keep as much weight as possible off the slight woman.

"I'm not going to break," she sighed impatiently.

I wasn't too sure of that.

After closing the door firmly in Conall's face, and refusing to acknowledge that I had an audience, I did what I needed to do. As I washed my hands, I looked at my reflection in the mirror above the sink, my aunt standing behind me with her hands on my waist.

"This didn't work out the way we were hoping it would, did it?"

Flora leaned back and scrubbed her hands down her face. "I wish we'd had a choice."

I turned to face my aunt. "What are you talking about? We did have a choice. I could have run. I chose not to." Despite how much I didn't want to, I had a feeling I was going to need to revisit that decision.

Flora shook her head and pulled a privacy stone out of her pocket and activated the spell. Considering the only werewolf in hearing distance was the one who would normally be a part of this discussion, I was a little surprised. "I had a vision of what would happen if you ran."

From the expression on her face I wasn't sure whether I wanted an answer to my next question. "How bad?"

Flora hesitated as if speaking it aloud would make it come true. "Conall will die protecting you."

The color drained out of my face and I started feeling faint again. Flora grabbed my shoulders and sat me down on the toilet after flipping down the lid.

I looked up at her, tears swimming in my eyes. "Conall's going to die?"

The pain from the arrow was nothing compared to what was happening to me now. We may have been having our issues but the thought of him not being by my side was devastating.

Flora cupped my chin in her hand and forced me to look up. "It was a vision, not a Seer's prophecy. Visions are meant as warnings. It won't necessarily come true."

It wasn't much hope, but I was going to reach out and grab it.

"That's why you pushed to announce it," I guessed. I'd been surprised at Flora's sudden turnaround in exposing my curse breaking ability, but I figured she had her reasons. I'd been right.

"I knew losing your Destined Beloved would break you in ways the Conclave never would be able to. I hoped they would show some restraint. I was wrong."

Something that had been bothering me pushed through the bone chilling fear that had gripped me at the thought of losing Conall.

"Are we sure it was the Conclave?" My mind started racing. "Just because Liam was a magister doesn't necessarily mean he was just reporting to the Conclave." I drew in a breath and started remembering some of my interminably boring lessons with Arthur. "The Conclave isn't necessarily a single entity. Isn't it made up of different factions which don't necessarily agree on everything?"

Flora nodded. "You're right. Immediately jumping to the Conclave doesn't take into account the bureaucracy of witch politics. I can't see them moving this fast or decisively. The original decision to kill the cursebreakers took years to implement. For them to put in place a course of action so quickly after our announcement is surprising to say the least. Even if they got the information directly from Magister Rigby, they wouldn't have been able to act so quickly. I would think we are more likely to be dealing with a lone wolf or a small group within the Conclave. Maybe even someone completely separate."

I guess that was some good news. My mind started racing with the possibilities.

"The sheriff is going to insist that you run."

Flora's quiet voice broke through the silence in the small room and I sighed.

"I won't do anything that puts him at risk of dying," I replied. "Don't even ask me to do that."

Flora closed her eyes. "No matter what course of action you take, there will always be that risk."

"Maybe, but your vision said that if we ran, he'd die, so we're taking that option completely off the table."

I watched Flora as she tried to decide whether it was worth fighting with me on this one. I saw the moment she accepted the futility of arguing when she gave me a sharp nod.

"We make our stand here."

At least we had a plan.

A tentative knock on the door interrupted us and Conall's voice came through. "Is everything okay in there?"

"We're fine," I croaked. "Just give us a second."

"Marigold needs to change your dressing."

I looked up at my aunt. "You know he's going to want to hide me away."

Flora nodded.

"I'm going to need your support to talk him out of it."

"You will have it."

Satisfied that I wasn't going to have to aggravate a berserker werewolf on my own, I pushed myself up, pain making the process slow. Flora opened the door and I didn't get a chance to protest before I was once again swept up into Conall's arms. He walked me over to the bed, gently laying me on it. I had a feeling we were going to need to have a talk in our near future. I was not going to be able to take this level of attentiveness for very long.

Once I was settled, the coven healer who had been watching the fussing I was receiving from the sheriff with great amusement, stepped up beside the bed.

"I'm going to remove the poultice and put some of the healing salve on. That should help with the closing of the wound. It will minimize the scar." She put on a bright smile. "In a few days you'll barely be able to tell that anything happened at all."

I felt the tension in Conall's hand as it gripped me tightly. I had a feeling that it was going to take more than some witch's magic, no matter how impressive, for my Destined Beloved to forget the last few days.

Marigold looked up. "We're going to need some privacy, so if you could just step outside…" Her voice trailed off as she got a good look at the expression on Conall's face.

"I'm not going anywhere."

"Don't be ridiculous," I hissed. "You can stay just outside the door. I will be perfectly safe in here."

"I'll go outside," Flora interrupted. "I know you will be fine."

She smiled at Conall as if expecting him to be as rational as she was being. I could see that Flora was trying to be helpful, but I could have told her that if she was expecting him to be reasonable, she was going to be very disappointed.

Flora slipped out of the room while Marigold and I turned to the sheriff.

"I'm not leaving."

I had a feeling that there was nothing more stubborn than a berserker werewolf, especially one who had just had the scare of his life.

I glanced over at Marigold and could see that she wasn't willing to take my side and play the medical professional card.

"Fine," I grumbled, "but you need to turn around."

"As you wish," he said as he stepped away from the bed and faced the wall.

"Let's get this done," I muttered to a confused Marigold.

I could tell she was having trouble understanding our dynamic. According to legend, a Destined Beloved prophecy described the ultimate in soul mates. As Conall and I were finding out, legends had a tendency to gloss over common human frailties. We were doing the best we could with an unusual situation.

As Marigold pulled back the hospital gown my nose wrinkled at the odor coming from the poultice packed on my chest. As she scraped away the mass, I got a chance to see the damage underneath. For a moment I flashed back to the feeling of the arrow piercing my chest and the look of horror on Arthur's face as he caught me and lowered me to the ground. I gritted my teeth to prevent the whimper of distress that I could feel wanted to come loose. Marigold stopped the scraping and I glanced up to find her looking at me.

"You're going to be okay," she whispered.

I blinked back the tears that were welling in my eyes and gave her a grateful smile. I nodded to let her know that I was ready for her to continue. She finished the process of cleaning up the poultice and then started slathering on the salve. At least it smelled a lot better than the poultice had.

"I'm finished," she remarked as she pulled the hospital gown closed. "Do you need anything?"

"How about some discharge papers?" I asked hopefully.

Marigold laughed. "Nice try. The doctor is the one who will be making that decision."

"You are not going anywhere until Collias gives you a clean bill of health," Conall muttered as Marigold left us alone. "I don't think you're realizing how close we came to losing you. I still have no idea how you survived."

I could see the distress in his eyes and the fear that we had just delayed the inevitable. I grasped his hand and brought it to my lips and kissed it. "You have me. I'm safe. I'm not going anywhere."

Before he could answer, the door opened, and he swung around. Flora slammed the door shut and leaned against it, raising an eyebrow at the gun that had seemed to magically appear in the sheriff's hand and was now pointed straight at her.

"If you're so keen to shoot somebody, I would suggest you start with the woman on the other side of this door."

Conall put the gun back in its holster. It still amazed me that, despite the fact we were in a paranormal town, the cops still had guns.

"If Collette's being a problem, I could have her arrested and held for twenty-four hours," Conall said as if that was a perfectly reasonable response to the situation.

What was worse was that I could see Flora was giving his suggestion some serious consideration.

"You are not arresting Collette Harstone," I said, unsure why I needed to be the voice of reason in this situation.

"You're right," Flora sighed as she turned to me. "She

wants to speak to you, and I don't think she's going to leave until she gets what she wants."

I drew in a shaky breath and glanced over at Conall who looked like he was a hair's breadth from tossing me in a bunker and slamming the door shut. "Fine, let her in."

9

"*Y*ou don't look like a Harstone."

I had to bite my tongue to prevent myself from informing the woman claiming to be my grandmother that I was thrilled with that observation.

"Sadie is a Harstone. I have confirmed it."

I couldn't help but feel for Flora. Over the last few months the two of us had created our own little family and we were happy with that. Collette Harstone had the potential to do a lot of damage. I was not going to allow that to happen.

"Oh, I know. We had her DNA compared to Jasper's. She is definitely his," Collette replied, disappointment coloring her voice.

I could feel Conall's hand squeezing mine as if to comfort me for the lack of a heartwarming reunion with my grandmother.

"How did you get my DNA?"

I had been repeatedly told that Flora had used her magic to claim me as a member of her family and that DNA testing wasn't necessary. I had become convinced it wasn't even a thing in the paranormal world. As far as first words to the grandmother I never knew I had, I couldn't say they were great, but I needed to know who was working against me.

She looked down her nose at me. "I still have friends in this town. You would be surprised how easy it is to get a DNA sample." She glared at Flora. "There was no way I was going to accept your pronouncement when it came to something as important as the Harstone family bloodline."

I could see that Flora and Conall were struggling with the way Collette was treating me, but I felt separate from the entire process. Throughout my childhood you would have expected that I would have some interest in my father and his family. I hadn't. My mother had explained the situation surrounding my conception when I was quite young. Even at that age I'd been able to understand the character of a man who would bolt in the middle of the night after a one-night stand while his partner was still asleep. My mother had pulled no punches with her explanation. I took the time as Flora and Collette sniped at each other in a way that only sisters could, to really look at this woman who should have held an important position in my life. As I studied her, I came to a conclusion. She was…unremarkable. That surprised me. After the stories that I'd heard about Collette Harstone, I had expected a woman who physically dominated the space she was in. Instead, I found an average older woman staring at me with piercing brown eyes. I was relieved to be able to say that she looked nothing like me. It seemed despite the supposed reverence that the Harstone genes were held to in the paranormal world, the normal Goodwin genes had beaten them into submission when it came to me. Knowing my mother, that had been deliberate. Everyone had always told me I looked like my mother. As a teenager I had hated that comparison, but as an adult prepared to face a side of her family that she wasn't at all interested in, I was grateful for that fact.

"What do you want?" My voice cut through the conversation that was happening around me.

Collette gave me what I was sure was supposed to be an ingratiating smile. "I'm your grandmother, and you have been hurt. Where else would I be?"

"I'm guessing anywhere but here," I replied.

Collette frowned at my response. "Your father was worried about you."

I snorted and then gasped at the pain in my chest at the movement. Conall started and I could see from the pinched look on his face that he was desperate to fix this situation but had no idea what to do.

I took a calming breath and looked Collette Harstone in the eye. I did not want her to misinterpret anything that I was saying. "At no time did I ask for you to come here. I have made no effort to reach out to you or your son, even though I was made aware of your existence months ago. That should give you some indication of my feelings on the matter."

"Surely, you want to meet your father. I can facilitate that." Collette looked as if she was holding the entire deck. Unfortunately for her, I wasn't interested in playing the game.

"Your son contributed the grand total of one cell to my existence. I am my mother's daughter. I have no interest in claiming the Harstone name. You never have to worry about me sullying it."

"It's too late for that, Cursebreaker," Collette sneered.

And now we were at the reason for this sudden flood of grandmotherly concern. Before I could answer another voice joined the conversation.

"I'm guessing this is a bad time, but I really don't care."

For the first time since Collette Harstone walked into my room, I smiled.

"Tilda."

My friend stood at the doorway, a grief-stricken expression on her face.

I lifted my hand and waved my fingers. "Hi."

"If this is a bad time…" I could tell that Tilda was trying to be diplomatic in the face of the Harstone drama. I was just happy for the interruption. Nothing was going to be gained from me continuing a conversation with Collette.

I waved my friend in. "We were just finishing up." I caught Collette's eyes. "Flora's sister just dropped in to ensure that I was okay. She has now seen that I am so there is no need for her to stay."

From the look of anger I got from Collette, I had a pretty good idea that she was not used to being dismissed, but I didn't care. We were never going to have a heartwarming family reunion. She knew what I was, and I had a pretty good idea what she was. Now, I figured it was best that we went to our separate corners of the paranormal world and never saw each other again.

"Are you telling me that you aren't interested in getting to know your father?"

"Not even a little bit." I raised my head and looked her directly in the eyes. I didn't want there to be any misinterpretation about what I was saying. "As far as I'm concerned, I have no father and there is no need to pursue the fantasy that I have."

I could see that my response was not what she was expecting.

"Very well," she said in a way that let me know that this was not the last I was going to hear from her. "I will give you time to recover from your trauma. Maybe then you will be more reasonable."

She swept out of the room.

"She really doesn't know you at all, does she?"

I laughed and then groaned at Tilda's insightful comment as pain shot through my chest again.

I looked over at Flora and caught the sorrowful look in her eyes.

"I'm sorry," I said. "I know she's your family, but I'm not interested in having anything to do with them."

Flora gave me a slight smile that didn't reach her eyes. "I'm the sister she never cared for who stole her destiny. Our relationship is always going to be colored by those events."

Silence descended on the room.

"Can I give you a hug?" Tilda asked, a plaintive tone in her voice. "I'm controlling myself here, but I really need to give you a hug."

I held my arms out and she smiled as she stepped towards me, only to be stopped by the arm of an overprotective berserker werewolf.

"You need to be very gentle," Conall growled.

Tilda rolled her eyes. "Because I was planning on body slamming her."

Conall pulled his arm back with some reluctance and Tilda gave me the gentlest of hugs. "I was so scared," she whispered.

"I'm okay," I reassured her. "Just might take a bit of time before I can keep up with you."

Tilda snorted. "Sure, I'm the problem."

She pulled herself up and sat on the edge of the bed before indicating to the sheriff. "At least you're looking better than he does."

For the first time I really looked at Conall. Tilda was right. According to the doctor he hadn't left my side since I'd been shot and that had been five days ago. That kind of stress was going to leave a mark.

"You need to go home and get some rest," I said, perfectly well aware of the response I was going to get.

"I'm not leaving you," he growled as he settled back in the chair.

I sighed in exasperation. "It's not about leaving me. If you don't get some rest very soon, you are not going to be any good to anybody. Despite what you may believe, you are not invincible."

Conall raised an eyebrow and I inwardly groaned at his cockiness.

"I'll stay with her for a few hours and you can get some sleep," Tilda interrupted. She wrinkled her nose. "You could also do with a shower."

Trust Tilda to lack the tact the rest of us had been showing.

Conall frowned at Tilda. "I don't understand why Eamon is so besotted with you."

"She's right, though," I said as I reached for his hand. "I know you've been taking care of me, but you need to take care of yourself. I'm not naive enough to think that things are going to get better, especially not with Collette hanging around. For at least the next few days I'm going to need you to be at the top of your game."

He studied me for a couple of seconds, and I could see the moment when he decided to listen. He stood and leaned over me, brushing his lips against my forehead. "I'm going to organize a deputy for the door. Nobody will be able to come in until I get back."

I grinned. "That should make Dr Collias happy. He looks like the kind of person who will take well to being ordered around in his own clinic."

"He was almost as worried about you as I was. Trust me when I say that he will do whatever it takes to keep you safe."

After the sheriff left Flora turned to me. "I should go too. I need to get some idea why Collette is really here."

"You mean she's not here to provide love and support for her wounded granddaughter," I said. "Color me shocked."

Flora gave me the first real smile I'd seen for the day. "It's good to see your attitude is still intact."

At the moment, my attitude was the only thing I had that still worked. My body felt like I had no strength in me at all.

"I'll be back in a couple of hours." Flora looked pointedly at Tilda. "You take care of her."

Tilda snapped out a salute. "I will protect her with my life, oh fearless leader."

Flora sighed with exasperation and headed for the door.

"You enjoy messing with her, don't you?" I remarked once the door was closed.

Tilda shrugged. "She's been wound really tight since you got shot. Now that we know you're going to be okay she needs to start unwinding fast or else she is going to explode on someone. I'd be willing to bet that someone is going to be Collette, and that won't end well for anybody."

I moved slightly to try to relieve the aching pain that seemed to be radiating throughout my body. "I'm just glad we managed to get Conall to have a rest. He wasn't looking good."

Tilda nodded. "I spoke to Karl and he said that the sheriff lost it when he was called to Old Man McClune's place and found you with an arrow sticking out of your body."

I grimaced at the visual I was getting.

"He hasn't left your side the entire time and he's been snarling at anyone who came near you," she continued. "Eamon was getting really worried about him. At one point..." She paused and I could see the shine of unshed tears in her eyes. "That first night, Collias didn't think you were going to make it and he told us to prepare ourselves. I really thought the sheriff was going to change into that berserker thing and kill everybody. He was right on the edge. I think the only thing that stopped him was the fact you were still breathing, even though it was really light. If you had stopped breathing, it would have been carnage."

I swallowed as I imagined the scene.

"I never want to go through something like that again," Tilda said softly. "I don't think any of us will cope if we lose you."

I peered at Tilda, desperate to pull her out of the emotional spiral she was talking herself into. "So, you and Eamon have been…"

"We've been talking," Tilda said. "Nothing else. I'm not ready for anything else." She looked around the room as if embarrassed. "I trusted Liam. I thought he might be the one for me. I can't believe my instincts could be so wrong. I don't want to make that kind of mistake again."

I reached out and patted her hand. "You won't," I said, my voice full of confidence. "I have a really good feeling about Eamon."

Tilda covered my hand with hers. "I hope you're right."

I couldn't believe that it took another six days before Dr Collias was willing to let me leave the clinic. I assumed that once I was conscious it would be all systems go, my remaining hospital stay only a matter of hours. It seemed my doctor thought differently. Unfortunately, he wasn't the only one who had conditions on my leaving the clinic.

"Please tell me, you're not serious."

It seemed that from the stubborn set of his jaw that the sheriff of Walker Bay was very serious. I reached out and poked at the vest he was holding.

"There is no way I can wear that." The thing had to weigh a ton.

"Somebody shot you with an arrow," he said through gritted teeth that seemed to indicate that I was forgetting that important fact.

"I remember," I replied, just as annoyed. "That doesn't mean that I should wear something that looks like it was the height of fashion in the fifteenth century.

It seriously did look like something out of a history book.

"This is the only thing that can stop the sort of arrow that someone who is trying to kill you is using."

"Do you really think that whoever did this has been hanging around for almost two weeks, while you've been coordinating the world's greatest manhunt, only to take a shot using the same weapon that failed the first time?"

I could see he wasn't going to be swayed by my logic.

"Fine, put the damn thing on me." I could have kept arguing but I knew that he would keep us there until he could get me to agree. After almost two weeks, I wanted out of this clinic in the worst way possible.

I stood there as Conall strapped me in.

"Oh, that's a good look." I glared at Tilda as she walked in the door, a wide smile on her face. "Let me take a wild stab in the dark here and guess that this outfit is not your idea."

I did not return her smile. "You think?"

Conall stepped back and nodded appreciatively as he examined his handiwork. I went to take a step and staggered under the weight of the vest. After almost two weeks confined to a hospital bed, it was a fair bet that my muscle tone wasn't what it used to be, or at least that was the excuse I was going to use. Both Conall and Tilda stepped forward and put their arms under mine as if to hold me up.

"I'm okay," I said. "It's just really heavy."

Conall nodded. "You'll get used to it. In no time at all you'll barely notice it."

Tilda caught the expression on my face and coughed to cover the laugh I knew she was hiding at my predicament. There was no way that I was going to be wearing this contraption long enough to get used to it. I just needed to get home before I had that argument with the sheriff so, with a wisdom I didn't realize I possessed, I decided to change the subject before we got into a discussion that was going to delay my discharge yet again.

"I'm starving. I've barely had anything to eat all day waiting for Dr Collias to finally decide that he was willing to let me go. I can't believe he waited until it was dark before he finally gave the okay."

"He's worried," Conall said softly. "And he knows you'll be less of a target at night."

I hadn't thought about that. It was fortunate that I had other people more skilled in dealing with the kind of people who would shoot somebody with a poisoned arrow. I had a feeling my life expectancy would be a lot shorter if I was left to my own devices.

"Do you want to go to the diner and have something to eat?" Tilda asked, purposely ignoring the man next to me who had stiffened at what I knew he would think was a reckless suggestion.

I looked down at my ensemble of sweats and armor-plated vest. "I don't really think I'm appropriately dressed for an evening out. Do you?"

Tilda grinned. "You might have a point. Would you like me to grab a couple of pizzas and meet you at home?"

"I would love you forever if you did that," I replied, my mouth watering at the thought of food that hadn't been nutritionally examined to maximize the healing process.

Conall rolled his eyes but didn't bother to object. It looked like both of us were learning to pick our battles. That had to be considered progress.

I ALMOST PUSHED my way past Conall when he finally opened the door to my house.

"I need to check it," he grumbled as he held me back from charging inside.

I waited impatiently just inside the door as he went

through every corner of my home before finally declaring it safe.

"Can you take this thing off me, now?" I asked as I drummed my fingers on the hard steel which surrounded me.

"My pleasure," he grinned as he started undoing the buckles.

"This isn't like the vests that normal cops wear, is it?" I asked.

Conall shook his head. "No, you were pretty close when you guessed it was from the fifteenth century. It's a normal steel combined with a bit of magic to protect the wearer from projectiles. It was the only thing I could find that was guaranteed to keep you safe if your assailant decides to take another shot at you with an arrow."

I sighed with relief as he slid the contraption off me. "You know I can't wear that on an ongoing basis," I said quietly as he laid it down on the floor.

"I know," Conall replied as he stood and faced me, his hands stroking down my arms.

I had noticed that he had become very tactile since I'd been shot, as if trying to convince himself that I was still here. I could see he wanted to hold me but was still a bit tentative about what he could do without hurting me. I took the initiative and stepped forward, wrapping my arms around his waist as I pulled him close. I felt him shudder at the contact and, despite his need to treat me gently, the hold he had on me was strong.

He lowered his forehead to mine. "That can never happen again," he said as if he was warning the universe.

I really hoped the universe was listening.

WHILE WE WERE LOST in our own world together, my front door flew open and Conall spun around, pushing me behind him.

"You're losing your touch, Sheriff," commented Tilda as she walked past us and placed the pizza boxes on the table. "You should have heard me before I even came close to getting to the front door."

Conall gave a rueful smile. "I'm a little distracted today."

"Understandable," she replied as she started pulling out plates as if she belonged in my house. "I would suggest paying a bit more attention. I could have been anyone."

I grabbed a plate and loaded it with a meal that was the complete opposite of what my doctor had recommended before I was discharged. "As far as I can remember you're the only person who has no problem with walking into my house without knocking." I gestured at the sheriff. "Except for him."

Tilda took a bite out of her pizza. "I probably should stop doing that, shouldn't I?"

"That would make me happier," muttered Conall.

Tilda dropped her uneaten pizza on her plate. "There's something that I think you should know."

That didn't sound good. Tilda's expression had turned serious. While I was in hospital, Tilda had made it her mission to keep conversation as light as possible. It seemed that she believed that if I was sufficiently entertained I would heal better. From her serious expression I could tell that I was not going to be entertained by the news she wanted to give me.

"I ran into Collette while I was picking up the food."

"Is she still around?" I chewed thoughtfully. "I thought she left days ago."

I hadn't seen my grandmother since the day she visited me in the hospital. When nobody mentioned her again, I assumed that my lack of enthusiasm for family ties had encouraged her to return home.

"It seems the Harstone family is returning to Walker Bay."

I swallowed hard as my food seemed to stick in my throat. "What do you mean?"

I could feel Conall's hand had dropped to my leg as if he could help control the panic that was coursing through me.

Tilda's voice gentled. "She told me the entire family arrived today."

I stood up suddenly and started pacing. This was not what I was expecting to have happen. I thought I'd made my feelings on the Harstone family clear. Never in a million years did I think they would be returning to Walker Bay.

"How many?"

Tilda shrugged. "She didn't give me much in the way of details. To be perfectly honest, I think the only reason she was telling me was so that the news would get to you. She knows we're friends. This is probably just a shot across the bow to see how you would react to the situation." She watched as I twisted my hands together. "First indications are that you're not dealing well."

I stopped pacing and tried to take in a deep breath. I could see that both Conall and Tilda were worried, but they didn't make a move towards me to try to comfort me. It seemed they knew me well. There was nothing that could comfort me in this situation. I thought I'd handled everything that had been thrown my way in the last few months with at least a little dignity and grace. Even though the hits had kept coming, I had coped and tried to calmly accept what was happening to me, up to and including getting a poisoned arrow in my chest. I don't know what it said about me that finding out my family was moving into the town I lived in was the event that was going to push me over the edge.

"How long are they going to be here?"

Tilda shrugged. "I don't know. She just said that the Harstones were returning to Walker Bay. They've opened up Harstone Manor and they are all moving in there."

"Harstone Manor?" I croaked.

Tilda pointed her hand north—or it could have been south—I'd never been good with directions. "Harstone Manor is that big mansion about ten minutes outside of town. It's where the Harstones have always lived. When Collette and the rest of the family left, they magically sealed it up in a petty move to ensure Flora could never use it." Tilda snorted. "Not that she ever wanted to. Flora moved out of that house the second she could."

I frowned. How had I not known this? You would have thought that at some point somebody would have pointed out that there was a family mansion. Not that I would have wanted anything to do with it. I had fallen in love with my renovator's delight at first sight and nothing was going to make me leave it.

Conall crossed over to me and grasped my hands. "It will be okay. You don't need to have anything to do with them if you don't want to."

I leaned forward and rested my head against his chest. "I'm just not ready to deal with this. I don't understand why they are here."

"You're a cursebreaker," Tilda said simply. "For a curse-breaker to appear now...it's like an extinct animal has randomly reappeared. You don't understand what a monumental moment in our history this is." She dragged her hand down her face. "Whatever the reason for them coming back, you can be sure that it isn't for anyone's benefit but their own."

I pulled out of Conall's arms and sat back down at the table. "I guess there isn't anything I can do about it." I looked over at Conall. "Unless you have the power to run them out of town." I couldn't hide the hopeful note that was in my voice.

"If I had the power to run somebody out of town just because I didn't like them, do you really think your ex-boyfriend would be living in the house next door?"

He had a point. I ate the rest of my meal in silence. Conall and Tilda kept up the conversation, but I couldn't help but notice the worried glances they kept throwing in my direction. I'd spent my whole life with the only family being my mother. After I came to Walker Bay, I had slipped into the habit of thinking of Flora as my only family. I knew there were others out there, not least of all Collette and Jasper, it was just easier to accept that they would never be a part of my life. I'd known when I threw my lot in with Flora that I was ensuring that I'd be outcast by the rest of the Harstones. Frankly, I hadn't cared. Flora had shown me love and acceptance that I hadn't felt since my mother died. Having anything to do with the rest of the family felt like a betrayal of what she'd done for me. Now it seemed they were determined to force their way into my life. I wasn't too thrilled with the idea.

Tilda stood up abruptly. "I think it's time for me to get going."

"What...?" I really hadn't been paying attention. I was going to blame it on whatever medications Collias had put me on. It had reached the point where I no longer knew which ones were FDA approved and which ones were just as likely to turn me into a toad with a little tweaking.

Tilda leaned over and gave me a hug. "I think you need some time to process everything and I have a feeling that I'm not the person you need to help you through this crisis." She glanced meaningfully at the sheriff who was watching me with a concerned expression.

I walked Tilda out and leaned back against the door after I closed it. I shut my eyes and took the first deep breath I'd been able to do in almost two weeks. The twinge in my chest was worth breathing in the scents of home, although, now that I concentrated, the place smelled a bit musty. I was going to need to air it out.

"You okay?"

I opened my eyes to find Conall watching me with that same worried look he'd had on his face since the moment I'd woken up. I hated being the cause of so much stress for him.

"I think I need to get some sleep. I'm really looking forward to spending some time in my own bed."

"Good idea. You weren't sleeping well at the clinic."

I stepped forward and started clearing away the remains of our dinner.

Conall watched me for a few seconds and then walked towards the front door.

I raised my hand, surprised at the abrupt way he was leaving. "I'll see you tomorrow."

He stopped and turned around. "It concerns me that you believe that I would leave you home alone when there is some psycho out to kill you."

I rolled my eyes. "I assumed that you would have organized some protection for me. That doesn't necessarily mean that it has to be you."

"It always has to be me," he said softly.

My breath caught at the naked emotion on his face.

His expression shuttered and he gave me a quick grin. "At least this time you'll know that someone is sleeping on your couch when you come downstairs."

I studied him carefully. During my stay at the clinic, Conall had barely left my side. The times he had succumbed to Tilda's and Flora's bullying and gone home for some rest had been few and far between, and you could see the signs of every sleepless night on his face. As I tried to ignore the fluttering in my stomach, I made a decision.

"You're not sleeping on the couch. If you insist on staying with me, you can sleep in the bed."

Conall's eyes widened with surprise. "Your bed?"

"It is the only bed in the house."

"With you?"

"I'm pretty sure the doctor would frown on me sleeping on the couch." It seemed he was having a little trouble understanding what was going on. "Don't panic, I'm not going to jump you," I said dryly. "I just think we both need a good sleep, and I have a feeling that we'd both sleep a lot better if we were within arm's length of each other."

He blanked the expression on his face, but it wasn't fast enough to hide the joy at my admission. "Okay, I'm just going to grab my bag out of the truck."

As I waited for him to come back, I realized that this was the first time I had been alone since I got shot. I swallowed at the sick feeling that seemed to crash through me. I was scared and I had no idea how to cope with the emotions. In the clinic I was so focused on healing and getting home that I hadn't given the idea that I had somebody hunting me much thought. Now it was all I could think about.

"Are you okay?"

I jumped at the sound of Conall's voice. He was frowning at me from the doorway. Usually I would have brushed his concerns off by telling him I was fine. I just couldn't get the words out so I shook my head. He dropped his duffle bag and strode over to me, gently pulling me into his arms.

"You're safe here," he said. "I'm not going to let anything happen to you."

The part of me that was so terrified I felt like I wanted to throw up clung to his assurance. If there was one thing I knew about Conall, it was that he took his role as my protector very seriously.

"The Harstones returning to Walker Bay is not a good thing, is it?"

"Nothing we can't handle," Conall said as he tightened his hold on me.

I closed my eyes and basked in the warmth and security he provided. I really hoped he was right.

$\mathscr{I}$ woke to the soft pressure of Conall kissing me on the forehead. I opened my eyes to find him standing over me. I frowned when I noticed that he was in uniform.

"What's going on?"

"I've got to go into work. I'll try to get back as soon as possible."

He gave me another quick kiss and left before my sleep-addled brain could catch up with what was going on. By the time I was able to form a coherent thought I heard the front door slam shut. That was surprising. I honestly thought I was going to need a stick of dynamite to dislodge that man from my side. I knew he'd been chafing to get back in the field and go after whoever shot me, but I hadn't expected him to leave me unprotected while he went hunting.

It took me a few minutes before I pulled myself together enough to make my way downstairs. I paused at the bottom of the stairs and tried to understand what I was seeing.

"It's about time you got up. I thought I was going to have to drag you kicking and screaming out of the bed. Do you realize that you do not have a single thing in this house worth eating for breakfast?"

I scrubbed my eyes just to make sure I wasn't still in dreamland. "Pike?"

Deputy Beastpike wrinkled his nose when he opened the refrigerator. "I'm pretty sure we're going to have to cordon off this area as a biohazard."

"I haven't been home the last two weeks due to getting an arrow in the chest." I was amazed that I could say those words so calmly. "I'll go to the diner and grab something to eat."

Pike snorted as he pulled out his phone, fingers flying as he texted somebody. "Yeah, you're not going out in public any time soon. I just contacted Tilda. She'll be bringing our breakfast to us."

Now I was confused. "What are you doing here?"

Pike settled in the chair and leaned back, his arms stretched wide. "I'm going to make sure that nothing happens to you. Think of me as your bodyguard. I'm going to be with you everywhere you go. I'm going to protect you with my life and make sure nobody messes with you. Just try not to get that psychological transference thing where you fall in love with the guy who's willing to take a bullet for you. That would be awkward."

I paused for a moment as my brain tried to keep up with all the things that he was saying. "Please don't take a bullet for me."

"It's not my primary plan," Pike drawled, "but it would put me in good with the sheriff. If I took a bullet for you, he'd never be able to fire me, no matter what I did."

I really didn't like the way that Pike seemed to be contemplating that scenario as a positive career move, so I tried another tack.

"Aren't you supposed to be working?"

"I am working," he grumbled. "Considering the trouble you have a tendency to get yourself into, I will definitely be working."

After a few seconds of confusion as I tried to understand precisely what was going on, I took a step back and pointed towards the stairs. "Okay, I'm going back upstairs to have a shower and get dressed."

I raced into my bedroom and grabbed my phone off the bedside table. I was grateful that the one person who could answer my questions had the good sense to pick up the phone on the first ring. Unfortunately, that was the only good sense the sheriff was showing today. Before I could say a word, he jumped in.

"You don't have a choice. I need to chase down whoever did this to you and I can't be in two places at once. You need protection so I can do my job."

It's like the man had spent time preparing a speech for this precise moment.

"Why have you assigned Pike as my bodyguard?" I hissed into the phone. "I'm not saying that it isn't a sweet gesture, but this is a misuse of police resources. You will be crucified for this."

"Pike took leave this morning. Technically speaking, he's on vacation."

"Then why is he…?"

"I would say that the most recalcitrant and anti-social member of my staff is not willing to risk losing you and has appointed himself your bodyguard."

My heart melted just a little. Nothing about Deputy Beastpike screamed sentimental but it seemed he had a soft spot.

"Don't say anything," warned Conall. "He won't cope if you go all mushy on him."

I knew that but I could still feel mushy about him.

Conall drew in a deep breath. "Please listen to what he has to say. I know he comes across as if his life's work is to cause destruction and mayhem, but he is very good at his job. Considering the number of complaints on his file, he'd have to be."

I wasn't even going to bother asking what kind of complaints he was talking about. I already knew Pike's personality well enough to take a wild guess.

"Please, Sadie. Despite the work that has gone into this investigation, we are still no closer to finding who did this to you than we were when you were shot. If we don't start getting some clues soon, we may lose any chance at tracking them down. Believe me when I say that I wouldn't have left your side for any other reason."

I could hear the stress in his voice. As sheriff of Walker Bay and as my Destined Beloved I hated to imagine the strain that he was putting himself under.

"I'll stay with Pike," I said, quietly.

"And do whatever he says," Conall replied.

"Let's not get crazy, here," I warned. "This is Pike we're talking about. I reserve the right to apply common sense to some of his more extreme ideas for my protection."

Conall sighed heavily. "Fine. I'll accept that but I want you to contact me at any time if you think I'm needed."

"Would that be before or after Pike uses a stun gun on some poor unsuspecting werewolf that looks at me the wrong way?"

"I have full confidence that Deputy Beastpike will conduct himself with the utmost professionalism," Conall stated.

At least one of us could say that with what I presume was a straight face.

12

*W*ith Sheriff Tolan's endorsement of my bodyguard ringing in my ears, I very quickly had a shower and got ready for the day. I was hoping to go to work at the library. I wanted to get a better idea about the slaughter of the cursebreakers and the coven library was the best place for me to start. If someone had decided to restart the genocide, with me as the first victim, I wanted all the information I could get. I just needed to talk my bodyguard into going, without telling his boss that I wanted to leave the house. It was fortunate that I had the bodyguard least likely to slavishly follow the rules.

I came down the steps to find Pike had decided to take his life into his hands and tackle my refrigerator. I was about to interrupt him when I heard a knock at the door. Without thinking I walked over and pulled it open.

"It's about time. I'm star...You're not Tilda."

I got shoved aside by an annoyed dwarf. "I know we didn't discuss rules yet, but I thought this one was self-evident. You do not answer the door," Pike growled as he stood in front of me, his hand twitching at the stun gun that seemed to always be on his hip.

"I'm not here to cause any problems." Julian Bernauer held his hands up as if he knew that the man standing in front of me was not one who was open to negotiation. "I just want to talk to Sadie."

Pike squinted at the magister. "I'm thinking that you're the last person the sheriff wants talking to her."

"Good thing he knows better than to make decisions for her," Julian said, talking directly to me.

"Well played," I replied. "Appealing to my sense of independence in the hope that it would be enough to convince me to do something that we all know would give Conall a coronary. Lucky for everybody involved, you're a little transparent and the whole arrow in the chest thing has given me a whole new appreciation of the sheriff's point of view when it comes to magisters."

Julian started to drop his hands to his hips.

"Nah uh, sunshine," Pike growled. "You keep those hands where I can see them. You make any sudden moves and I'm going to make sure that you're dancing like a monkey." He tapped the stun gun. "I've given this baby some extra juice and it should provide some serious entertainment." Without taking his eyes off the magister he nodded in my direction. "Speaking of which, pull out your phone. If I need to shoot him, I at least want to get some footage for an after-action report."

I wish I could tell if he was serious or not. "You are not going to shoot a magister just because you want to test your weapon. I don't think even the sheriff would approve of that one."

"You'd be surprised," Pike muttered.

Ignoring him I turned to Julian. "What do you want?"

"I wanted to see you when you got shot but the sheriff wouldn't allow me anywhere near you."

"Considering you were probably somewhere close to the top of his suspect list, I'm not surprised," I said, refusing to disagree with the decisions Conall made on my behalf when I was at my most vulnerable.

Julian started lowering his hands again but changed his mind when Pike glared at him. "I want you to know I had nothing to do with your shooting."

How weird had my life become that my ex-boyfriend felt the need to tell me that.

"How about your fiancée?" Pike asked the question that had been on the tip of my tongue.

Julian ignored the question. "Who are you and why are you even a part of this conversation?"

Pike puffed out his chest. "I'm her protector."

Julian looked at me with amazement as if he doubted Pike's abilities. I knew better. What Pike lacked in stature, he more than made up for in naked aggression and an uncanny ability to find a person's weakest spot and exploit it.

"The Conclave did not do this."

Julian's absolute statement surprised me.

"That's a pretty big claim you're making there."

Julian nodded. "I know you find it hard to believe, but I have been assured that the Conclave would not take any action that would be detrimental to the peace that they have built up with the other paranormal races. They are very aware of the interest that the Assembly has taken in your case."

"So, who do you think did it?" I asked.

"What do you mean?" Julian seemed confused by my abrupt question.

"You're saying that it's not the Conclave, even though the

method of the attack screams Conclave involvement. If you truly believe they are innocent, who do you think did it?"

"I wish I knew. If I did, you can be assured that they would never come after you again." Julian raised his eyes and I could see the haunted look in them. "Please believe me."

Before I could reply Pike interrupted. "Those are pretty words, Magister, but you and your fiancée still top the suspect list. If you really want to help the investigation, I suggest you get your butt over to the sheriff's office and actually do something useful rather than just spout flowery words."

Julian waited to see if I had something to add. When I remained silent, he nodded sadly. "I would never hurt you."

He probably would have said more but Pike was bored with the conversation and slammed the door shut in his face.

"I don't think that was the best way to handle that particular situation," I remarked.

Pike shrugged in a way that indicated that he really didn't care. "Do you believe him?"

"I have no idea. I would hope he's telling the truth, but I'm not quite ready to bet my life on it."

Pike nodded in agreement. "I don't know why you keep insisting on talking to him. You do realize that as far as you are concerned, he is the enemy?"

"What's that saying about keeping your friends close and your enemies closer?"

Pike gave me a smile that straddled the line between endearing and evil. "I prefer to roast my enemies over a spit and then bury them at the bottom of a very dark hole, but that could just be me."

There was a loud knock on the door. Pike and I looked at each other.

"He's a lot dumber than he looks, isn't he?" Pike asked conversationally as he pulled the stun gun out of his holster.

"Please don't shoot him," I pleaded.

Pike reached for the door. "A smart man would only need to be told once. I was very clear. Whatever happens next is the result of some defect in his personality. Let's call it an opportunity for character development."

I reached for him as he pulled open the door and pointed the stun gun at a shocked Tilda.

"Are you out of your mind?" she shrieked as she jerked her hands up, barely holding onto the bags of food that she was carrying.

Pike quickly holstered his weapon. "Sorry, thought you were somebody else."

Tilda and I watched as he relieved her of the food and carried it to the table.

"Please tell me his being here is only a temporary measure," she muttered as she stepped through the doorway and stopped next to me.

"I wish I could," I replied as I held my hand up, my fingers an inch apart. "He's been protecting me for a grand total of an hour, and he was this close to taking out a magister."

"I'm never sure whether I should be grateful he's on our side," Tilda mused.

I could understand that thinking.

"Will you ladies please hurry up," Pike said as he pulled containers out of the bags and spread them across the table. "A man could starve to death waiting for the two of you."

Wondering how long Pike was going to deem it necessary to shadow my every move, and whether the general public was going to survive his interpretation of what my protection required, I sat down at the table and gratefully tucked in to the bacon and egg wrap that Tilda had thoughtfully brought me. She sat down next to me, keeping a wary eye on Pike.

"What are you planning on doing today?" Tilda asked when she finally started to relax.

"I'm thinking of going into work," I replied.

I could feel tension build in the room at my announcement. Fortunately, Pike had his mouth full of a breakfast burrito and had obviously been taught by his mother not to talk with his mouth full because Tilda was able to jump in before him, showing a level of tact that was simply beyond the deputy.

"Do you think that's the best plan for today? Wouldn't it be better if you stayed in the house and just give the sheriff a little more time to chase down the person who almost killed you less than two weeks ago?"

I almost felt bad when I heard the pleading tone in her voice. My guess was that Conall had lectured all my friends that I was supposed to be kept as safe as possible. "I'm not going to sit idly by while everyone else tries to solve this," I held up my hand to forestall the argument. "I was the one who was shot. I can't just wait for everybody else to solve this problem. I'm only going to the library to get some information. The fact that whoever did this used an arrow with an ancient poison to try to kill me has to mean something. I'm hoping there will be a book in the library that will give some clue as to where the poison comes from. If we can track that down, then we may be able to find the person who would have access to it."

Pike cocked his head to one side. "That's not the worst idea I've ever heard," he commented. "The coven library is a defendable place. We can keep the threat contained and as long as we—and by we I mean you—don't do anything stupid, it shouldn't be too much of a problem."

I was going to take that as a ringing endorsement, but Tilda still didn't look convinced.

"It'll be fine," I assured her. I was going to say more but at that moment the front door swung open again and, showing a speed I did not know he possessed, Pike sprang up and swung around, his stun gun clearing the holster in a move that was almost superhuman.

This time it was Tilda and I who screeched when Flora came into view. Tilda even managed to throw herself in front of the coven leader, in a move that was a great deal less graceful than Pike's had been.

Fortunately, Pike's reflexes were razor sharp and his brain had registered Flora's presence before his trigger finger had engaged. He had holstered the weapon, sat back down at the table and continued eating his breakfast burrito before the echoes of our screams had died down.

I dropped my head and sucked in a lungful of air as I tried to calm down the adrenaline that had flooded my system at the thought of Pike sending volts of electricity coursing through my great-aunt's body. Tilda seemed to have stopped breathing altogether and had dropped to the floor once the danger was over. I walked over and squatted down next to her.

"Are you okay?"

Tilda shook her head. "I think I just lost a full decade of my life," she muttered.

"Does somebody want to explain to me what just happened?" Flora looked perplexed as she watched me patting Tilda on the back.

"We're all just a little on edge," I said as I helped Tilda to her feet, pleased that I only felt a minor twinge in my chest.

"You need to knock next time you wish to enter this house," Pike stated.

Flora's eyes narrowed. "This is my niece's home. It is up to her whether I need to knock or not."

Great. "I think you should start knocking," I said. "Just for the short term at least. Less chance of an unfortunate accident happening that way."

From the expression on Flora's face I could see that she wasn't happy with my decision, but I preferred her to be annoyed rather than a victim of Pike's seemingly overwhelming need to make every situation so much worse.

"Would you like some breakfast?" I gestured towards the table.

"No, thank you." She paused as if searching for something to say. "You look a lot better." She gestured to my face. "You've got some color in your cheeks."

I took a seat. I had never seen a rambling Flora before. I could tell from her voice and the way she was wringing her hands that something was wrong. I had a feeling I was going to want to be seated when I found out what it was.

"What's going on?" I asked, completely sure I wasn't going to like the answer.

"You and I have been summoned to Harstone Manor for dinner tonight." Flora smiled as if relieved to have got that out of the way.

"Summoned?" I really didn't like that word and the Goodwin side of me was having an instinctive reaction to refuse based on that word alone.

Flora nodded as she pulled out a chair and sat down. "As head of the Harstones, Collette has the right to summon any member of the family to her presence."

"I don't think that's such a great idea." Both Pike and Tilda were nodding furiously in agreement with me.

"Unfortunately, we don't have a choice," Flora replied. "She made it an official summoning. If we don't attend, we will give her grounds to officially cast us out of the family."

I was failing to see the bad side of that outcome and my expression must have reflected what I was thinking.

"I don't believe alienating the family would be the best

way to go." Flora's voice may have been quiet but the steel running through it challenged me to disagree. I sighed inwardly. Just because I had no use for the Harstone family didn't mean that Flora was the same. She'd been a thirteen-year-old child when she had effectively lost her family through no fault of her own. I could understand that there was a part of her that was desperate for the kind of relationship with her sisters that she thought she should have. I glanced over at Tilda. She knew I was going to capitulate. That didn't mean that we didn't have some sticky issues to deal with. Fortunately, Pike brought up the biggest of them.

"The sheriff is never going to agree to her walking into that viper's nest without him," he growled.

Flora grimaced. "Sheriff Tolan has been given permission to accompany his Destined Beloved to the dinner," she said formally, her constantly moving hands the only sign of the stress this situation was putting her under.

I had never seen Flora like this. She had always been the calm and competent coven leader. We had faced any number of terrifying situations and she had been my rock. It seemed we'd found her one weak spot. That was not good.

"Does Conall know?" I asked.

Flora nodded. "I've already spoken to him. He's not thrilled with the idea, but he's willing to see it from my point of view." She reached out and grabbed my hand. "Collette is a member of the Conclave and she wields enormous power in our world. If she can begin to feel even the slightest bit of family loyalty to you, we will have an invaluable ally in the fight to protect you. Nobody will touch you if you have Collette standing with you."

I could see what she was saying. I just didn't want to agree with it. I had no reason to trust any of the Harstones and there was a part of me that was terrified of the idea of meeting them. I could handle Collette. I just couldn't handle...

"Will Jasper be there?" I was proud of the fact that my words were steady. Most of me had no interest in meeting the man who fathered me, but there was a small part that was unsure. I'd never really thought about Jasper Harstone as a father. The few facts I knew about him didn't really give me any confidence that I'd missed out by not having him in my life. It was why I'd never made any effort to find out about him or to track him down.

Flora nodded and I took in a few deep breaths. I could do this. He was a minor footnote in my history, that I would be meeting for dinner tonight. I felt my heart thumping in my chest. This may be a problem.

"What time is this dinner?"

For the first time since she walked in the door Flora smiled. It was more of a relieved smile than a happy one, but at least she'd stopped wringing her hands. "Please get there by seven. I'll be arriving a little earlier so you won't have to face them alone."

I guess that was something.

"*N*ew plan," I announced after Flora had left after dropping her bombshell. "If I'm walking into the lion's den tonight then I'm going to need all the information I can get on the Harstones. I need a better source than the library."

"Flora just left," Tilda pointed out.

I shook my head. "Not Flora. Her opinions are going to be colored by being abandoned by her sisters while she was still a child. You saw what she was like just telling me about the dinner. I don't care how much you think you've dealt with family issues. That kind of trauma is going to leave a mark and I'm not going to make her dissect the ones that hurt her." I paused and looked at Pike. I knew my next suggestion was not going to be well received. "If anybody knows what I'm going to be facing tonight, it's going to be McClune."

Tilda put her hands on the table and pushed herself up. "And I'm out of here."

I frowned, a little confused at the sudden turn of events. I had thought that Tilda would be the last person I needed to convince of the rightness of my plan. "Surely you don't have issues with him."

Tilda was one of the most well-liked members of the Walker Bay community. You had to work hard to find somebody willing to say a bad word about her. I thought she could get along with anybody.

She shook her head, a determined expression on her face. "I would just prefer that I didn't exist to him. He kind of had a starring role in most of the ghost stories told when I was a kid. Let's just say that I'm not particularly fond of the idea of finding out how close to reality those stories were."

Now that I thought about it, the less people I dumped on McClune the better. I frowned as I imagined his reaction when Pike turned up.

"Don't even think about it," the dwarf in question said calmly.

"Think about what?" I should have known better. A lot of people underestimated Pike and didn't look past his thuggish behavior. You'd think by now I would know better.

"You're thinking that it would be preferable that I didn't go with you either." He raised an eyebrow. "That is never going to happen."

Tilda put up her hand as if she was in class. "I don't want to be the voice of reason here, but have either of you given any thought to how the sheriff is going to react to you returning to the place where you were shot?"

Believe it or not, I had. It didn't take a genius to work out that he would be very unhappy. Fortunately for me, he had chosen to leave me with the deputy least likely to care about following the rules as my bodyguard. If he hadn't realized there would be consequences to that decision, then that was his mistake.

I could see in Tilda's eyes the moment she realized that nothing she said was going to change my mind. She surprised me by leaning down and giving me a quick hug. "Just don't do anything stupid, and let the sheriff know what you're doing. After the last couple of weeks, he doesn't deserve the extra stress."

I smiled up at the woman who had become the closest friend I'd ever had. Despite her words, I knew she would come with me if I asked it of her, despite her fears. "Don't worry, I've got Pike."

From the expression on her face I could tell that statement did not make her feel any better.

AFTER TILDA LEFT, I turned to the most important task at hand. Explaining this situation to the sheriff without giving him any reason to come running to my side. I won't say that somebody was looking out for me when I got the no service signal, but I wasn't willing to look a gift horse in the mouth. It seemed that even in a world of magic, phone companies still weren't able to provide a decent product. I sent a quick text in the hope that he would receive it when he moved to an area that had reception.

"Ready to go?" I asked Pike. I had to say that I was a little surprised that he hadn't voiced one word of objection to my plans for the day.

"Whatever you want."

I turned back to the deputy. "If you have something to say, just say it. This silent thing you have going on doesn't fit you."

Pike leaned back against the couch and crossed his arms. "I'm just waiting for you to realize exactly what you're doing."

I had no idea what he was talking about. He sighed at the confused expression on my face. "You really think that Tilda refused to go to McClune's place because of some horror stories from when she was a kid?"

It sounded logical to me.

He shook his head as if he couldn't believe he was having to explain something to me. "She knows that she won't be able to cope with going to the place where you almost died without breaking down. We came so close to losing you. It scarred everybody in some way. Tilda's hiding her scars by being bubbly and friendly, but she knows the second that she steps on that property, she's not going to be able to hide the gut-wrenching fear that's churning up inside of her. The sheriff is burying himself in the hunt. I'm unwilling to leave your side." His voice was soft as he proved once again why everybody underestimated him. "And you are trying to plan out your day so you are busy with anything else and you don't have to think about the fact that you are absolutely terrified."

I could feel my mouth going dry. He was right. On the second day of being confined to the clinic I had started to be overwhelmed by the fear that seemed to creep into every part of me. I'd reacted the same way I had whenever I had been paralyzed by my emotions. I'd made plans and deliberately thought about anything else rather than what had happened to me. In my mind I'd renovated my house and made decisions about policies I'd wanted to bring into the coven library. Now Pike was trying to strip the comfort I'd found away from me.

"Don't do this," I whispered. "If you take this away from me I won't be able to function."

Pike eyed me keenly as if trying to decide how far he could push this. When he reached a decision, he nodded. "Very well. I'll leave it alone, but you are going to need to deal with this, or it is going to take you to your knees at a time you least expect it."

I breathed a sigh of relief and worked at concentrating on what kind of information I was hoping to get from McClune. The emotion that had gripped me around the throat started to recede at the realization that I had another day when I wasn't going to have to deal with what happened to me.

Pike forced a smile. "Fair warning, last time I was on Arthur McClune's property, I may or may not have accidentally set something on fire."

14

⚓

J kept a tight leash on my emotions as we drove up to the McClune place. I could do this. I refused to walk into Harstone Manor without at least some background knowledge and I had a feeling Arthur McClune was the person who could help me. I wasn't surprised when he hadn't turned up to the clinic to check on me. That wasn't the sort of person he was. It was enough that he had managed to get medical help to me quickly enough to save my life. I owed him. I had a feeling that knowledge was going to make him insufferable.

We found Old Man McClune waiting on the porch of his house when we pulled up, as if he knew that it would only be a matter of time before I returned.

"Come inside," he motioned when we got out of the car.

I stopped as shock speared through me. Despite the number of times I had come out to the place, I had never been invited inside his home. We had always gone to the clearing beside the river that flowed through his property. The same clearing where I had been shot. I unconsciously rubbed at my chest. Pike bumped into me. I looked down at him, annoyed at his actions until I noticed that his head was swiveling. Of course, while I was feeling privileged at being permitted inside McClune's house, my bodyguard was trying to ensure there wasn't a repeat of the shooting. I let him hustle me inside the building.

I wished I could say that I was surprised at the spartan condition of McClune's home. There was almost nothing that indicated that a person lived here and had lived here for decades. From what I could see there was a main room which consisted of a small kitchen and living area with one door leading off of it. I assumed that was to a bedroom. The whole effect made me incredibly sad. No wonder he always made us go to the river. Compared to the stark emptiness of this building, the river would be the only place that would feed his soul.

"Take a seat," he said as he indicated a couple of very old chairs. I sat down tenderly, not at all sure that it would hold my weight. I noticed that Pike ignored the suggestion and planted himself to the side of the front window, peering out into the forest.

"What can I do for you?"

And that was Arthur McClune in a nutshell. I'd almost died in his arms, but now that I was sitting in front of him he didn't feel any need to ask me how I was or what I was feeling. The proof was in front of him. Anything he said or asked was just words, not relevant to why I'd sought him out.

"The Harstone family is back in Walker Bay."

He raised an eyebrow as if to let me know I wasn't telling him something he didn't already know.

"Flora and I have been summoned to Harstone Manor this evening. I need to know what I'm walking into."

McClune leaned back in his chair. "You don't believe that this is simply a family wanting to welcome a lost lamb back into the fold?"

I gave an indelicate snort. "I know you think I'm an idiot sometimes, and given some of the questions I ask you that is a safe assumption to make. One thing I know is that Collette and Jasper would not be here if I hadn't been outed as a cursebreaker."

McClune stroked his hand down his silvery beard. "At least you don't seem to be harboring fantasies of a loving reunion. That gives you a fighting chance of getting through this situation with the least amount of damage possible."

"I need to know everything about the Harstones and what motivates them."

"Power," McClune said simply. "Harstones have always been motivated by the lust for power."

I frowned at the bold statement. "That doesn't sound like Flora."

"You're right," he replied. "Flora was always very different from the rest of her family. She never sought the leadership of the coven. It was thrust upon her. You also need to remember that she shared a different father to her sisters. Maybe his genetic influence muted the Harstone characteristics."

I thought about what he said. "What about me? I'm a Harstone but I don't think I'm motivated by power."

"Being brought up in the outside world means that your life has been very different. I'm guessing your mother had a very strong influence on the woman you've become."

He wasn't wrong. My mom had taken on the role of mother and father, and she had excelled at both.

"Jasper was never even close to being a strong Harstone," McClune mused. "Chances are the other side of your genes overwhelmed his."

I was pretty sure that wasn't the way genetics worked. It was probably a good thing that I was here to learn about history and not science.

"Tell me about Collette," I urged.

McClune smiled but it wasn't a nice one. "The one thing you need to know about the Harstones is that they never strive for power on their own. It is always a family matter. The most important thing you need to know about power. It's not the one at the front who's blustering and ego driven that you need to worry about. It's the people behind the throne, the ones whispering in their ear. They are the ones that destroy the world."

"What are you talking about?" I couldn't help the frustration in my voice. I needed information now.

McClune took a deep breath. "We can't talk about Collette without knowing about Dinah's role in her ambition."

"Dinah is Flora's other sister?" I confirmed. Since I'd arrived in Walker Bay, I had heard plenty of things about Collette. I hadn't heard much about Dinah. At times I had wondered why that was.

McClune nodded. "Collette and Dinah Harstone were as close as two siblings could be. They lived their whole lives believing that Collette would be taking over the coven, and Dinah would be at her side. For hundreds of years there have been two females born to each Harstone generation. One is in the spotlight and takes the position of power and one stays in the background. In most cases the second one becomes the more dangerous of the two. The thing you need to remember is that they are completely loyal to each other."

I frowned as I did the math. "But there were three females in their generation."

"I know." McClune sighed heavily. "Based on Harstone history there shouldn't have been. We're talking generations. Before Collette and Dinah, there was your great-grandmother Bessie and her sister, Amelie. Before them there was your great-great-grandmother, Alice, and her cousin,

Clementine. I could take you back hundreds of years and it will always be the same. Two girls in each generation, all in a perfect line, all with one goal in mind—to seize power and hold it. Walker Bay has always been a center of power for the paranormal world. To be coven leader here is to have a strong voice in the Conclave, if you want it."

"But Flora doesn't want that voice."

"No," McClune replied. "Flora has never sought power for herself. What she has always wanted was to keep her coven safe. Nothing is more important to her than protecting those she cares about." He paused. "If Bessie's pregnancy and the birth of Flora had not been quite so public, I would have doubted that she was even a Harstone."

I tried to take it all in. "So, what you're telling me is that the Harstone family was perfectly uniform until two generations ago when everything went off course, culminating in Collette losing out on the leadership of the coven." I frowned as a thought occurred to me. "If the Harstones are all about power, why did Bessie step down from her position as coven leader. She was still relatively young, wasn't she?"

McClune nodded approvingly. "You see things quickly. That will stand you in good stead. Amelie died quite suddenly several years earlier, and Bessie never recovered. The coven suffered due to her grief. I know that local legend has it that the coven split due to Flora being given the leadership position, but that's not entirely true. The seeds were sown in that period of time between Amelie's death and Flora becoming coven leader."

"And that's when the Path coven came into being?"

McClune stood up and started pacing as if he had a surplus of energy to get rid of. "Do you think the Path coven is new? Versions of it have been popping up all through history. Discontent with the status quo will always find fertile ground somewhere. For a period of several years the

Harstones lost their tight grip on power in Walker Bay while Bessie wallowed in her grief. Somebody was always going to step into that breach. In this case it was the Path coven. I don't think the coven split because of any great loyalty to Collette, despite what they say. I think it split because it was always meant to. Those witches who left were just looking for an excuse which would allow them to not make an enemy of Collette and Dinah." McClune eyed me carefully. "The last thing anyone wanted was to be considered an enemy of those two women. They still keep to the public avowal that Flora usurped the role of coven leader, but mark my words, they are far happier to be dealing with her kinder form of governance, rather than the iron control that would have occurred if Collette and Dinah had taken power."

None of what McClune was telling me was making me feel any better about what I was walking into this evening.

"Why did they leave?" I asked. "I know everyone believes that the Seer's prophecy was absolute, but you can't tell me that two strong women as obsessed with power as those two would have let a thirteen-year-old girl get in their way.

McClune raised an eyebrow. "Normally I would have agreed with you, but I think that Collette and Dinah decided to take the opportunity."

"How?"

"The leadership of the Walker Bay coven has given the Harstones power, but it has also been a trap. While they were based here, they couldn't extend their influence."

Slowly, the confusion cleared. "They made a play for the Conclave."

"Yes," McClune replied. "They had allies and it didn't take long for Collette to receive a junior position. Since she took her seat on the Conclave she has moved very quickly towards a position of power."

"Do you believe it was her or Dinah who masterminded this?"

"Dinah," McClune said with certainty. "Don't get me wrong, Collette is a strong woman, driven by ambition, but Dinah is capable of being truly ruthless. The problem is because she is in the background, you won't see her until she strikes."

"You've got a lovely family there," Pike drawled. "Are we absolutely sure the DNA test is accurate, because if there is any wiggle room at all, I'd be jumping on it."

I truly wished that was a possibility.

"What about their children?" I asked. "I know Jasper is Collette's child, but I haven't heard of any others. If there's supposed to be two women in that generation to take over power, who are they?"

"Collette only had Jasper. My understanding is that she was desperate for more children, even shedding more than one husband in the pursuit, but she was not blessed."

"And Dinah?"

The elderly man settled back down on the chair. "Dinah had twin girls."

"So, there are two," I murmured.

"There were two," McClune corrected. "Evaline survived the birth but Eugenie was stillborn."

"Did she have any others?" I asked.

I was surprised by the look of sympathy on the older man's face. Considering his attitude to the Harstones I found it unexpected. "The birth was hard. She was unable to have any more children."

Now I could understand the sympathy. "So, no second female in that generation."

McClune nodded sadly. "Through history the Harstones have been nothing but predictable. Two women in each generation acted together as a force to be reckoned with.

Two generations ago, something started to change." He looked at me thoughtfully as he stroked his beard. "It may be worth wondering whether that change was needed to bring forth a cursebreaker."

"Really?" I couldn't stop the incredulous tone in my voice. "You're suggesting that Bessie Harstone having three daughters led to me being born this way?"

"I'm suggesting that in my lifetime I have found that random events don't just happen. Everything is linked, especially when it comes to beings of power."

I wasn't so sure.

"Is there anyone else I should be aware of?" I asked, fighting to keep the fatigue I was feeling from showing. I knew Pike was watching me like a hawk and his face was starting to show concern. I may not like the limitations that my injury had put on me, but that didn't mean that I could ignore them.

"Collette and Dinah have one surviving child each. Jasper is married and has two stepchildren."

I'd been so determined to never think of Jasper Harstone that the possibility that I might have siblings in this world had never occurred to me. "Do I have any other brothers or sisters?"

McClune shook his head. "As far as I have heard he hasn't had any other children of his own." He gave me a small smile. "Of course, until Flora told me about you, I thought he'd had no children at all. My understanding is he has never been the most responsible of men, so it is possible that you have any number of siblings out there. You just might need to go looking for them."

"What about Evaline?"

"Aah yes," McClune drawled. "Evaline is the reason that I originally thought the last two generations were an anomaly. She provided the Harstones with the requisite two girls."

"How old?" I asked, curiosity getting the better of me.

"They're both twenty-nine," he replied. "Along with their brother."

"Triplets?"

He nodded. "Before you came along it seemed that the Harstone family was back on track."

"And then I throw the whole cursebreaker thing into the mix."

"You've definitely made life more interesting."

"You've got that right," Pike agreed. He turned to me. "Have you got everything you need from here?"

I frowned at the sudden query. "I'm not sure. Why do you want to know?"

Pike motioned me over to the window. "Because I have a feeling that we've run out of time."

I looked through the window to see a furious sheriff heading in my direction. What shocked me was that he was accompanied by the magister I had barely managed to stop Pike from shooting earlier. Seemed Julian had taken Pike's advice to heart and offered his assistance in the hunt for my attacker. Or he was being arrested for the crime. From the look on Conall's face I couldn't really tell.

"Any chance we could hide in here?" I asked, pretty sure I knew what the answer was.

"You might want to check that optimistic streak of yours," Pike replied. "Sometimes I think you're tripping over into delusional territory."

"I sent him a text." I was starting to feel a bit defensive. I knew that when Conall went to work this morning, he'd expected me not to leave the house. You would have thought he'd know me better by now.

15

"*W*hat the hell are you doing here?" To say that Conall was angry didn't even come close to describing the emotions pouring off him. "You are supposed to let me know where you are at all times. "

"I sent you a text explaining this after I tried to call you." I frowned as I remembered something. "Anyway, I thought you had a locator beacon thing on me."

One of my least fond aspects of the Destined Beloved prophecy was Conall's ability to find me no matter where I was. He claimed he used it sparingly, but I had my suspicions, and from the sheepish look on his face I had a pretty good idea that he'd known exactly where I was.

"You almost got shot on this property," he gritted out. "Why would you come back?"

"Because I needed information that I could only find here," I replied. "We were inside the house the entire time and Pike kept watch. We made the situation as safe as we could."

I knew he wanted to argue with me, but he also needed to know that I wasn't going to let him make all the decisions.

Before he could start coming up with new arguments, I asked the obvious question.

"What are you two doing here?" I waved my hand between the two men.

Julian smiled at me in a way that seemed designed to irritate the sheriff. "I've offered my assistance in trying to see the assassin."

That made sense. Julian had once shown me his ability to bring the past back to life as if we were watching a movie. It was by far the coolest magical gift that I had seen so far. In my opinion it was definitely better than being a cursebreaker, but then I thought anything was.

"Is it okay if I watch?" I asked before thinking the request through.

"I don't think that's a great idea." Julian looked at Conall, expecting his support.

He was sadly disappointed when the sheriff dismissed his concerns. "They tried to kill her. If she wants to see their faces, that is her right."

Sometimes Conall Tolan surprised me.

"But you will do everything I say without argument," he growled, "and when we are finished you will go straight home."

And sometimes he didn't. I'd thought his anger had dissipated a little too quickly.

I looked back at McClune who was watching the scene unfolding in front of him with a little too much amusement. "Thank you for your help."

He quirked an eyebrow. "If you think I don't want to see who did this on my property, you are sadly mistaken.

Conall reached out a hand and gripped mine. "You stay close to me." His words had a chill to them, and I looked at him carefully. Despite all appearances I knew he wasn't coping well. Conall was a man whose life revolved around protecting the people of this town. The fact he'd been willing to accept Julian's help was proof that he was beginning to get desperate.

It didn't take long for us to reach the clearing by the river and, despite the warm sun, I shivered. Fortunately, time had erased my blood from the ground but that didn't take away the dark pall that seemed to hang over the area.

Conall's hand held mine more tightly as he stopped on the edge of the clearing. "You need to do your thing." He gestured towards Julian who was staring at the spot where I had fallen.

"Are you sure she should be here," Julian said hoarsely. "I cannot stress enough how unpleasant this is going to be for her."

Sometimes I underestimated how truly irritated Julian could make me. "She had to live through it," I bit out. "I'm pretty sure that whatever I'm about to see is nothing compared to the vivid images that go through my head every night."

Julian inclined his head as if conceding the argument. He then put his hands out and started chanting. Shadows in the clearing started to coalesce until I could make out the shadowy forms of me and McClune on the day I was shot. The conversation looked intense, but we couldn't hear it. I saw myself start to walk out of the clearing when McClune grabbed my arm and I started to turn back. It was at this point that the arrow came flying out of the trees and slammed into me causing me to fall against the old man. I could feel the tension in Conall as we watched McClune lower me to the ground. Seeing myself scream and trying to fight him off as he pushed down on the wound made my stomach churn. I'd somehow managed to suppress those images and I was beginning to see the wisdom behind Julian not wanting me to see this.

"Stop there!" Conall's voiced boomed in the quiet. "Take it back to when the arrow was shot."

The images ran back until a moment before the arrow hit me and then froze. I could see the effort it was causing Julian as sweat ran down his face. Conall let go of my hand and walked up to the image of the arrow suspended in mid-air. He looked over at me as if to see whether I realized the significance of the placement. The arrow was perfectly aimed for my chest. If it hadn't been for the sudden move- ment when McClune grabbed my arm, I wouldn't have had a chance against the wound, let alone the poison.

Conall started walking towards the trees, tracing the trajectory where the arrow had come from. Without a word we all followed him until he stopped.

"What is that?" I croaked. My mouth had gone dry at the sight in front of us. I had expected to see a person targeting me. What we saw was darkness. Wisps of blackness seemed to have surrounded whoever had shot the bow and completely blotted the person out.

"What is this, Bernauer?" the sheriff growled.

Julian's face which was already showing the strain he was under, paled. "That is the shooter," he replied.

"Then why can't we see them?"

"Because whoever did this is somebody who knew that I would eventually be assisting in the investigation. They were carrying a talisman that specifically wards against my ability."

"Can you do anything with it?" Conall asked.

"What part of 'targeting my abilities' did you not under- stand?" I winced at the sarcasm in Julian's voice. I didn't think he understood how close to the edge the sheriff was.

I was surprised when Conall didn't react. Instead he studied the dark shape.

"I can't hold it much longer," Julian panted, sweat pouring

down his face. "Whoever did this has put a sting in the tail that actively works against me."

Conall nodded in understanding. "Can you start it moving forward again? I want to see what the shooter does next."

The movie, if you could call it that, started playing again. The darkness made its way through the trees and we followed until it simply disappeared.

"That's all I can do," Julian gasped as he drew in shaky breaths. "I'm sorry I couldn't show you more."

Conall raised an eyebrow. "On the contrary, you've given us plenty. Now we know the path of the shooter, I'll get a team together to sweep this part of the forest. There is no way they came through here without leaving something of themselves behind." He looked down at me. "I need you to go home now."

I gritted my teeth to stop the first comment that went through my head to come flying out of my mouth.

"Of course." I glanced at our depleted magister who was being held up by the dwarf at his side. "I think I should take Julian home with me. He's not going to be any good to you like this."

I could see that Conall was not happy with my suggestion, but he was also too keen on following up on a possible trail to ignore the fact that he needed to have the magister taken care of.

After several moments when I figured his decision could go either way, I could see the moment that he capitulated. "Fine, take him back to his house so he can rest." He pulled me aside and lowered his voice to prevent anyone else from hearing. "You are to keep Pike with you at all times. I do not want you alone with Bernauer for any reason. I'm still not sure whether he's involved or not." He silenced me with a look when I opened my mouth to defend Julian. "It's a little convenient that whoever shot you knew exactly what to do to prevent Bernauer's ability from working properly. I don't believe in coincidences."

Despite my annoyance at what he was saying, I couldn't suppress the sliver of doubt that had always been in my mind about where Julian's loyalties would lie once I outed myself as a cursebreaker.

I nodded sharply and Conall brushed a kiss across my lips. "Stay safe, sweetheart. The world is full of people who seem to want to do you harm."

"And we're probably having dinner with several of them tonight," I reminded him.

Conall winced. "Yeah, Flora told me about the summoning. I did try to argue that it was a really bad idea, but she was being unusually stubborn."

I'm glad I wasn't the only one who had noticed that Flora was not reacting well to her family descending on Walker Bay.

"We're going to need to keep an eye on her," I murmured. "I think there's a part of her that has an idealized version of what a relationship between sisters should be, and she can't let go of the hope that one day she is going to have that relationship with them. If we're not careful, Collette and Dinah could use that yearning against her."

I looked up at Conall and was struck by the thoughtful expression on his face.

"The same could be said about you and your father."

I scoffed at the thought. "My circumstances are completely different. I have never had any illusions about the kind of man my father was, or the kind of relationship we could possibly have. I always knew that there was never going to be a happy ending there, even if I did get the chance to meet him."

I could see that Conall had no reply to that. He didn't

want to take away any hopes that I may have about finally meeting my father, but he was too much of a realist to attempt to sway me from my cynicism.

"Just be careful," he muttered. "There are too many unknowns right now. I'm having trouble trusting anyone's motivations at the moment."

He wasn't the only one. I stepped back. "I'll take Julian home and then Pike and I will stay in the house until you get there," I said, figuring I should do something to make his life a little easier.

Conall smiled. "Just keep an eye out and listen to Pike. He'll keep you safe."

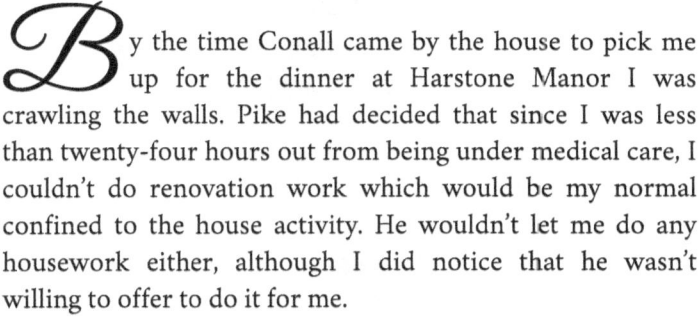

16

*B*y the time Conall came by the house to pick me up for the dinner at Harstone Manor I was crawling the walls. Pike had decided that since I was less than twenty-four hours out from being under medical care, I couldn't do renovation work which would be my normal confined to the house activity. He wouldn't let me do any housework either, although I did notice that he wasn't willing to offer to do it for me.

According to Pike, the only thing I was capable of doing was sitting on the couch and reading a book. I had a feeling that there had been strict instructions from the sheriff while we were at the McClune property.

Needless to say, I breathed a sigh of relief when Pike left the house. I could work around Conall. Trying to convince Pike of anything was like banging your head against a concrete wall. Repeatedly. More than a few times I had become convinced that he was going to pull out his stun gun and use it on me.

"You cannot leave Pike with me, again," I said before Conall could even say hello. "We're going to kill each other, and you're going to have to find yourself a new deputy and a new Destined Beloved. What are you smiling at?"

Conall didn't say a word. He wrapped his arms around me and then proceeded to kiss me thoroughly. When he lifted his head, he smiled. "You look stunning, my love."

I'm ashamed to say that my thought processes, which had been turned to mush by his very skillful kissing, melted into a complete puddle at the sweetness of his words.

"Thank you," I whispered. "You're looking pretty amazing yourself." He did. I didn't think I'd ever seen Conall in a suit, and I had to say I was enjoying the experience.

"So, we're definitely doing this?" he asked. "I couldn't convince you to do literally anything else?"

I grimaced at the query. I had to admit, during the interminable hours with Pike, I had been contemplating that very same question. The only reason I was subjecting myself to this dinner was because of Flora. I didn't care about the summoning or being turfed out of the Harstone family. It's not like I really belonged.

"We have to go," I sighed as I held my hand against his chest. The feel of his heartbeat under my fingers gave me strength. "How bad could it be?"

Conall snorted. "I'm going to remind you that you said that."

HARSTONE MANOR WAS a structure that was built to intimidate those about to enter it. In my case it was successful. My stomach churned. I did not want to be here.

Conall leaned over and tipped my chin until the only thing I could see were those pale blue eyes of his. "It's going to be alright. I won't leave your side and the second you want to leave, we will."

The front door opened, and Flora walked out. I frowned as I could almost feel the tension emanating from her.

"That does not look as if the initial portion of the evening has been going well," Conall muttered as he opened the car door.

I got out of the car and pretended not to see Conall's annoyance that I hadn't allowed him to play the part of the gentleman. I stepped over to my aunt and gave her a hug.

"Is everything okay?" I kept my voice low.

Flora patted me on the arm. "Of course, it is, my dear. Everybody's looking forward to meeting you. Let's not keep them waiting."

She turned away and headed back into the house. Conall stepped up beside me and grasped my hand.

"Did you see that smile on her face?" I muttered.

Conall nodded as he kept his eyes on the front door. "I'm thinking we should avoid whatever it is that she is drinking."

I tightened my hand on his. This was it. Any question that I might have ever had about my father and his family was about to be answered. I just couldn't understand why I seemed to be fighting the instinct to run.

"I will drive you anywhere you want to go. Walking through that door is your choice."

I looked into Conall's eyes, touched by his earnest offer. "You'd really do that for me, wouldn't you?"

Conall let me see the love that he kept professing in his eyes. "Haven't you worked it out, yet? I'd walk through fire for you. Taking you away from a dinner that I didn't want us to attend anyway doesn't even rate."

I reached up and brushed me lips against his. "Thank you," I said simply as tears welled in my eyes. One slid down my cheek and Conall wiped it away with his thumb.

"No tears," he whispered. "Don't let these people see one moment of weakness. We cannot trust any of them."

I took in a deep breath and straightened my shoulders. He was right. "Let's get this done."

Conall squeezed my hand and we started up the steps to the front door where Flora was patiently waiting for us.

"We're ready," I said as I straightened my shoulders and did my best to remove any expression at all from my face. I could do this.

Flora led us into the house and if I'd been even slightly less nervous my jaw would have dropped. It was unnerving to see the sheer opulence of this house, especially when I compared it to the plain house that Flora currently lived in. Her home seemed so normal. This place was as far from normal as you could possibly get.

"You used to live here?" I croaked.

Flora nodded. "Until I became coven leader," she replied. "After the rest of the family left Walker Bay, I needed to find other accommodation."

Just when I thought this family couldn't disappoint me anymore, they managed to set a new bar. Although, leaving a thirteen-year-old child homeless did seem like a special kind of low.

We followed Flora through the house and into a large room. My first thought was that there were far more people in here than I was expecting. In fact…

"What the…?"

Just when I thought that I had seen everything in this town that could shock me, I saw Aidan Tolan standing in the last place I would have ever expected to find him. My understanding was that Conall's father hated all witches—except for when he was having an illicit affair with them—and would not be caught dead accepting a dinner invitation from a member of the Conclave.

I glanced at Conall and could see that his jaw had

clenched tight. If he hadn't been fighting every instinct to drag me out of here before, he was definitely doing it now.

Flora looked guilty. "Maybe I should have told you before you came in."

"Oh, no, we absolutely love surprises," I replied, the sarcasm unmistakable in my tone.

I sighed at Flora's miserable face. This wasn't her fault, at least not all of it. I put an arm around her shoulder. For the first time since I met her she was uncertain and I wished there was something I could do for her, but I knew we were all going to need to face our emotional demons ourselves. Now that Aidan was here, that put Conall off his game as well. I frowned at the thought and wondered whether that was deliberate.

Collette broke from the group and came toward us. "Sadie, it is so good that you could join us. We've been looking forward to this moment for so long." She looked over at Conall. "Sheriff," she said with as much enthusiasm as if he'd stormed the place with a SWAT team, rather than being invited.

Conall inclined his head. "Ms Harstone."

Collette turned her back on him and smiled widely. She gestured towards a man who had been lounging on a chair and talking with Aidan. His hair was shot with gray and he had the glassy eyes of someone who had decided that a bit of dutch courage was needed to get through the night. I wasn't sure if that was a sign of weakness or intelligence.

"This is your father, Jasper. I can't tell you how much he has been looking forward to meeting you."

The fact that she could say those words without choking was further proof that Collette Harstone was a consummate politician. Anybody could tell that Jasper had no interest in being here, and even less interest in meeting me. I had a feeling that Collette kept a very tight rein on her son. Jasper held out his arms as if to hug me. My efforts to step back and avoid him were assisted by Conall putting an arm around my shoulder and pulling me into his side.

Jasper dropped his arms and put out a hand instead. I shook it and had to fight the temptation to wipe my hand when he let go. I hadn't expected to feel an instant connection to this man, but I had thought there would be something.

"I'm very pleased to meet you," he said as if by rote. "I have spent my whole life waiting for this moment."

He was trying desperately to play the role of caring father. Unfortunately, I was sure it was for his mother's benefit, not mine. As far as I knew, I had only been on the Harstone radar for the last few months. I couldn't see any way that he would have known about me before I ended up in Walker Bay.

"It's nice to meet you," I replied, unsure of what else I could say in this situation. I gestured towards the sheriff. "This is Conall Tolan."

Conall put out his hand and Jasper grasped it. I knew that I should have given more information in the introduction, but I really didn't know how to explain our Destined Beloved prophecy in a succinct way that made sense, especially to a man who I doubted believed that such a thing could exist. I couldn't help but notice that his eyes kept darting towards Collette as if he was looking for confirmation that he was doing what she expected of him.

An older woman came up next to Jasper and laid a hand on his arm as if to calm him down. In contrast to Jasper, there was no nervousness. I had a feeling that this was the woman Jasper had married. I had the disturbing thought that she reminded me a little too much of Collette. A young man and woman who looked very like her stepped up as if to reinforce that they were together.

Jasper awkwardly patted the woman's hand in what I think he saw as a gesture of affection. "This is my lovely wife, Sidonia." He gestured to the two young people standing close. "And this is your stepbrother, Tade, and your stepsister, Lorelei."

Sidonia gave me a smile that didn't reach her eyes. "We are so happy to welcome you to the family."

That was an outright lie. There was no way that Sidonia could hide the fact she wished I didn't exist and she was angry with her husband that this situation was even happening. Her children just seemed bored. To be perfectly honest, I couldn't understand why all these people had been gathered here at once. I knew that there had to be a reason for this large gathering, but I simply could not grasp what it was. I had trouble believing that these people were that desperate to welcome a half-normal cursebreaker into the illustrious Harstone clan.

After meeting Jasper and his family, Collette introduced me to her sister, Dinah. Most of the stories that I had heard about the Harstones had centered around Collette and her positions of power, but McClune's warning about the person behind the throne being the more dangerous kept ringing in my ears. Dinah had been the first person that had greeted me warmly and if I hadn't been pre-warned I may have overlooked the sharp intelligence in her eyes. I could see the way that she took in everything about Conall and me. I had a feeling that any conversation I had with her was going to end up with her discerning far more information about me than I would find out about her. Unlike her nephew, she was playing the situation perfectly. She introduced me to her daughter. Evaline looked to be a carbon copy of her mother and I could see the same awareness and ability to both read and manipulate a room. Recognizing my curiosity about the three young people who seemed to

be the same age as me, Dinah instantly started intro-
ductions.

"This is Malin and Rebecca, my granddaughters, which
would make them your second cousins, I think," she gushed
as she gestured for the two young women to come forward.
"And this is Elijah, my only grandson, thank goodness. I
don't think we could have coped with more than one of him."

Elijah rolled his eyes at his grandmother's attempt at a
joke. I had to admit, I was impressed. In only a couple of
minutes Dinah had managed to turn an extremely uncomfortable situation into something else entirely.

By the twinkling in her grandchildren's eyes, I could see
they were used to their grandmother's ways.

"Isn't this great?" Aidan boomed as he stepped up to the
group and flung an arm around Conall for what I suspected
was the first time in his life. "The two families coming
together for a meal, sharing all we have in common, looking
to our combined future."

Compared to Dinah's exquisite ability to read the room,
Aidan showed that he had a way of making any situation that
much worse. In a flash we were back to uncomfortable and
fake and, if I was reading Collette's expression correctly,
faintly nauseous. I caught the look on Conall's face before he
managed to erase it. At least I was no longer the only one
with an irrational overwhelming urge to run.

17

*R*ealizing that the chances of pleasant small talk were diminishing rapidly the more we tried it, Collette ushered us into the dining room. Conall very deliberately ignored the place holders which had separated us and sat down next to me. I smiled at the defiant way he caught Collette's eye. She was definitely not a fan. I hadn't expected her to be. On my other side I wasn't surprised when Dinah took her place. Jasper, who was originally the one who was supposed to be sitting in the seat Conall took, looked lost without explicit instructions on what he was supposed to do. In the end Sidonia took charge and pointed him to a seat opposite me. I had a feeling it was something she had to do often.

The meal began with servants bringing in a variety of dishes. If I hadn't been feeling nervous enough, this ramped that feeling through the roof. I was not a formal dinner and servants person. I was a grab a pizza and chat with friends while the dinner conversation became slightly inappropriate kind of person. I was so far out of my comfort zone it was ridiculous. I glanced at Conall and found that he seemed right at home. I copied his movements in the hope that I didn't look too out of place. If the Harstones were going to stay in Walker Bay, I had a feeling I was going to need lessons.

"Sadie, can you tell us about yourself?" Collette's voice cut through the low murmuring of separate conversations.

My mouth went dry at the knowledge that everybody was now focused on me. The only thing that stopped me from panicking was the reassuring pressure as Conall pressed his leg against mine. I smiled at him gratefully. I was beginning to realize that this man was always going to have my back, and right now I needed that.

"There's not much to tell," I croaked. "After my mother had me, we moved around a bit, following any job she could get. I had a normal childhood and when I got out of school I started working in a local library. That's pretty much where my career ended up going. A few months ago, Flora got ill and the leadership of the coven sought me out to help." I didn't add the obvious, that the only reason they went for the half-human rather than one of the powerful witches at this table was because Flora's family had all refused to provide assistance. By some of the uncomfortable expressions I could see around the table, they were all very aware of that piece of information.

"And how is your mother?" Jasper asked in an effort to change the subject.

I narrowed my eyes. These people had managed to surreptitiously get a DNA sample from me. You could not tell me that they hadn't done a simple background check.

"My mother passed away this last year," I replied, doing my best to answer the question with a calm I didn't feel.

From the look of disgust on Dinah's face, I had a feeling that Jasper had been told of my mother's death. He just hadn't cared enough to retain that piece of information.

"Oh, I'm sorry," Jasper stammered. "She was a lovely woman."

I raised an eyebrow at that statement. He had barely known my mother. I had a feeling if I asked him to give me her name, he wouldn't have been able to. I decided that little test would not be an appropriate use of my time. I also imagined it would be unseemly if I got so angry with my father that I stabbed him with a fork during the main course.

Conall, proving he knew me better than anyone, put his hand over mine as I gripped the fork.

"How have you found Walker Bay?" Dinah asked in a desperate attempt to take my attention away from her emotionally inept nephew.

"I love it," I said simply. "I have a house that I'm renovating and I plan to settle down here."

"The old Balfour place?" Collette asked.

"I have no idea who used to own it." I glanced at Flora, hoping she would help me seeing as she was the previous owner.

"That's the one," Flora agreed.

Collette frowned. " That place is a death trap."

"You're not the first person to say that," I replied. "The renovations are coming along slowly but I'm enjoying it."

"We could organize some help for you," Collette offered. "You shouldn't have to do it yourself."

I could see that she was trying to be helpful, but to me it seemed like she wanted to take something away from me that I wasn't willing to give up.

"I'm enjoying the work," I said, "and Conall does a lot of it as well, when he's not too busy."

Aidan snorted quietly. It seemed that the show of fatherly affection from earlier in the evening had stretched his acting abilities as far as they could go.

Conall squeezed my hand and when I looked up he slightly shook his head.

"How does the Destined Beloved prophecy work?" Malin asked, her eyes seemingly innocent of any guile. "I've never heard of one between a witch and a werewolf. Not that there's anything wrong with it," she said hastily. "I've just never heard of one."

I shrugged at the question. If she was looking for any great insight into the prophecy I was the last person to give it to her.

"It means we're a team." Fortunately, Conall had jumped in to answer the question. He was answering Malin, but he was looking at me. "No matter what stupid thing we do or how irritated we get, we know we'll always be there for each other. Nothing will ever change that."

I smiled at the earnest expression on his face.

"It's an abomination is what it is." It looked like Aidan had reached the end of his ability to act like a civilized human being.

"Tolan!" snapped Collette. "While you are a guest in this house, you will treat your son and my niece with the respect they deserve."

If it had been anybody else, they would have stepped back from the edge after a reprimand from a member of the Conclave. Of course, this was Aidan Tolan, the werewolf alpha. He was never going to bow to anybody. He stood up and swept his arm in a gesture encompassing everyone in the room.

"You cannot tell me that anybody at this table thinks for one moment that this is a good thing." He pointed at Conall and me and sneered. "A cursebreaker and a berserker. Neither of these things are supposed to exist. They are abominations in both our worlds." He glared at Conall. "I should have drowned you at birth, whelp."

That did it. I stood up and leaned forward, my hand still gripping that fork. "Your son is an amazing human being. I would say he is a credit to you but that would be assuming you had any positive contribution to his upbringing. He is the good man he is despite your presence in his life. I will not stand for you speaking like that to him."

I was angry. So very angry. I could feel something dark and twisted trying to break free. I clenched my jaw as I tried to rein in the ugly emotions coursing through me. The power seemed so close. A part of my mind whispered with ideas of how a cursebreaker could teach this upstart to never challenge me again.

Flora and Conall seemed to be the only ones at the table who could see that something was happening here that could end very badly. They both pushed their chairs back and took to their feet.

Conall wrapped an arm around my shoulders and pressed a kiss to my temple. "It's okay, my love. I don't care enough for his words to hurt me."

Flora reached my side and put a calming hand on me. "I'm right here. Tell me what you need."

I took in a deep breath and looked around as it was finally dawning on the other guests that this wasn't a simple case of a family spat, that something dark and dangerous was swirling around them.

"I think we need to go home," Conall announced, taking the decision out of my hands. "Sadie is still recovering from her injury. She needs rest."

I don't know why he even bothered to try using an excuse. Everyone could see that I was seconds away from losing it at Aidan. Only a few knew enough about curse-breakers to realize what that could possibly mean.

It didn't take long for Flora and Conall to hustle me into Conall's truck. "Please don't kill the werewolf alpha," Conall muttered as he buckled me in. "You have no idea the paper-work that would involve."

I couldn't help it. A small giggle escaped me.

Conall smiled. "And you're back. Thought I was going to lose you there for a second."

"I thought the same thing," I replied. I grabbed his hand and kissed it. "Thank you."

He turned my hand over and kissed me on the palm. "Thank you. Nobody has ever stood up to Aidan like that to protect me. You have no idea what it meant to me."

My eyes prickled with tears as I imagined Conall's miserable childhood trapped in a house with that man, and the anger started coming back.

Conall must have recognized it because he rushed around to the driver's side. Unfortunately, he wasn't quick enough as Collette knocked on my window and I wound it down.

"I'm so sorry," she said. "I thought having Aidan here would show we wanted to accept every part of your life. I should have known better." She shook her head. "We're your family and we want to be a part of your life. Please don't let this one incident push you away from us."

The words were the right ones, but I still didn't trust that the confrontation with Aidan hadn't been engineered for some reason.

I tried to swallow the lump in my throat. "I just need some time." I waved my hand. "This all seems to be a bit much and I'm having trouble taking it all in. I think everyone at once was a bit ambitious."

Collette nodded as if to convey her understanding. "Of course, everyone just wanted to meet you."

I had a little trouble believing that.

"Maybe later." I gave a wan smile as Conall started the truck in a not so subtle attempt to end the conversation.

"Of course," she said as she stepped back. She raised a

hand. "You are my only grandchild. Whatever makes you happy."

I waved as we drove off. "Do you think she means that?" I asked Conall.

"I don't know what to make of tonight," Conall replied. "If we get another invitation like that..."

"It was a summoning," I pointed out.

"I don't care what it was," Conall said. "We're not going to another. Not until we know exactly what it is that the Harstones want from you."

That was a decision I could get behind.

IT DIDN'T TAKE LONG for us to get back to my house and I smiled at the sense of peace I felt every time I walked through the door. I was surprised when Conall closed the door and gently pushed me against it. Before I had a chance to ask what he was doing, he dropped his head and crushed his lips to mine. Most of our kisses recently had been tender and coaxing. I knew that Conall was focused on marriage and it had seemed that he was trying to gently persuade me. This was a full assault on my senses. I was fortunate that his body was pressed against mine because I would have fallen to the floor as my legs gave out. He swept into my mouth and took control, demanding that I give him everything. My head spun and my hands gripped his shoulders, desperate for this feeling to never end. Just as I thought I would pass out from the emotions I was feeling he eased back.

"You have no idea how much I love you," he said.

I was beginning to understand. It wasn't the big gestures that mattered. It was what he did every day. He made sure I ate enough and got enough sleep. He was helping me renovate my beloved house when the consensus around town was that it should be bulldozed. He stayed at my side at the clinic, being my advocate when I was too weak to fight for myself. There was no way I would have been able to rest and heal without knowing he was watching over me. He left a slightly unhinged dwarf as my protector because he knew I needed to be safeguarded, but also knew I needed a bit of the craziness and hilarity that only Pike seemed to be able to provide.

Without a word I pushed away from the door and held out my hand. Hope and a hint of lust sparked in his eyes. I led him up the stairs. I'd finally reached the point where I wanted to make this prophecy real.

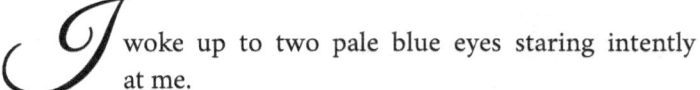

woke up to two pale blue eyes staring intently at me.

"You know," I yawned. "Some people might find that a little creepy." I stretched and smiled as I registered how alive my body felt. For a woman who got shot two weeks ago, I was feeling pretty damn good, and only part of that was due to the magical component of my healing regime. The rest of it was due to the very talented man in my bed.

"What's the time?" I asked as I squinted against the sun coming through the French doors.

"A little after nine," Conall replied.

"Really?" That was unusual. I hardly ever slept past dawn.

Conall grinned and I could see flashes of the arrogant werewolf in him. "We did have a very late night."

"That we did," I agreed as he stroked his hand down my side. "I would have thought you would have left for work by now."

"I'll get going, soon," he replied as he brushed some small kisses along my jawline. "I just need a little motivation before I head in."

I smiled. Motivation I could do.

~

IT TOOK us a bit longer to get ready than it usually did, but I couldn't find it in myself to worry about the rest of the world.

Conall gave me a long kiss at the front door. "I really have to go in to work."

I gave him another kiss. "I'd rather you stayed here with me."

Conall pulled away. "Trust me, that would be my first choice too, but we need you to be safe." He tucked some of my hair behind my ear. "Pike's on his way here. He should only be a couple of minutes. Stay inside and don't answer the door to anyone until he arrives."

"Fine, I'll be good," I said. "I am giving you fair warning though. I want to go into the library today."

"No," he said as the playful lover of the past twelve hours morphed back into the implacable sheriff who had still not worked out who had shot me. "It's too dangerous."

I sighed and wished I didn't need to have this argument. "How long do you think you're going to be able to keep me in lockdown?" I asked. "It's been two weeks. You can't keep up with this state of alert permanently. It's not healthy for either of us."

"It isn't going to be permanent," he growled. "It's just until we catch whoever did this."

I put a hand on his arm and I could feel the tension vibrating from his body. "I know you're going to find who did this, and I know you will do everything to protect me." I licked my lips nervously as I tried to work out the best way to put this. "I need to get information that only the library could have. It might have a clue about what is happening."

I watched as he considered what I was saying. "Fine, but Pike is to be with you at all times, and I need to be notified when you leave the house, and when you return."

"I can do that," I said and smiled. "Look at us, compromising like grown-ups."

Conall scowled. "Just let me take baby steps. I'm not used to people not doing what I say."

"That sounds healthy." I gave him a soft kiss. "Now get going before I decide that I don't want to let you leave."

Conall laughed as he put his hand on the doorknob but frowned when the door wouldn't open."

"What's wrong?" I asked.

"It's stuck," he replied. I could see the strain in his arms as he tried to pull the door open.

"Maybe the wood swelled because of the weather?" I was pretty sure that I'd read about that somewhere. "Try the back door."

I followed Conall and found that we had the same problem there. I could see the concern rising in his expression as he started trying to open windows.

"We could try the doors to the deck," I suggested.

We both headed upstairs, but this time we didn't make it past the bedroom door which slammed shut as we reached it.

"That was not the wind, was it?"

I don't even know why I asked the question. Despite the issues this house had, I had never been unable to get out of it.

"Can we kick down the door?" And by we, I meant Conall. I assumed he'd had practice at that kind of thing.

I glanced over to see him pulling out his phone as we headed downstairs. "Before we start damaging the house, I'm going to call Pike," he said. "Doors don't just jam like this. Something's not right here and I'd rather get some information regarding what's going on outside of the house before we start kicking through doors. For all we know there is somebody out there planning on picking us off the second we escape."

That was why he was the sheriff.

He stopped as if he had a thought. "Could it be a curse?"

I shook my head. "I can't see anything that would indicate that a curse is at play."

"But it's not a guarantee."

I had no idea. "There could be a curse outside the house causing this that I simply can't see."

Conall's phone started ringing. "It's Pike." He hit the answer button and put it on speaker.

"Do not come out of the house!"

I had never heard that kind of fear in Pike's voice. My heart sank as my mind started going through the possibilities of what could have caused it.

"Report!" the sheriff barked.

"There are wires on the front door."

"What?" I couldn't even think what that meant.

"Is there an explosive device?" Conall's voice was calm but his hand sought mine and squeezed it. My mind had locked up at the news.

"Yeah," Pike replied, his voice sounding as if he was out of breath. "It looks pretty crude, but I think it's designed to go off when the front door is opened."

"Then why weren't we able to open the door?" I asked. "If someone is trying to blow us up you wouldn't think they'd make it so we couldn't set it off."

"Transfer to a video call," Conall ordered. "I want to have a look at this thing."

It didn't take long for Pike to change calls. Conall and I peered at the phone screen and got the first look at the bomb that was attached to my house. Usually I would say that I knew nothing about the construction of a bomb and what was required to disarm it, but in this case I was uniquely qualified.

"In answer to the question that nobody asked as to whether I can see a curse through the magic of video, we have a yes. Nobody can touch that thing," I warned.

Conall dropped his head, the frustration rolling off him. "Let's get this straight. The front door is wired to explode, but there is a curse on the bomb that will go off on anyone who tries to disarm it. Does that sound right?"

When he put it like that, the situation sounded bad.

"What do you suggest we do?" The fact that Conall was looking to me for answers underscored just how much trouble we were in.

"You get me out there so I can break the curse before anybody tries to dismantle the bomb." I thought that was self-evident. "There has to be a way out of this house."

"I have tried every door and every window," Conall replied. "They're all shut tight. We could try to break one of the windows and get out that way."

"That's a good idea," Pike said as he panned the video to the front window. "From what I can see, this window's clear. Just smash something through it. Before I had time to understand what they were saying, Conall grabbed a chair and hauled it at the window. Instead of crashing through, the chair bounced back at us. Conall just barely managed to grab me and pull me down before I got taken out by the flying chair.

Conall hauled the two of us up and inspected the untouched window. "How did that happen?" he finally said. "That window should have shattered into a million pieces."

If he was looking for answers, I wasn't going to be able to help him. I had never seen anything like that before.

"Could it be Flora's wards?" I asked, wishing that I had a

better working knowledge of the magic I came into contact with on a daily basis.

Conall shrugged. "However it's happening, it means we have no way of getting out of here." He dragged his hand through his hair. "How were they able to do this without me noticing?" he snarled. "It happened during the night while we were in this house. I should have heard or at the very least smelled them."

Other than the fact we'd been pretty occupied last night, there was another possibility.

"If the bomb has been cursed, then we're looking at witches," I pointed out. "Is there a chance they could hide themselves from you while they were setting these using magic?"

Conall nodded. "It's a skill some witches have."

"Hold on a second," Pike said. "I'm going to get some help here." He looked at the bomb on the front door again. "You're sure I can't just yank the wires out?"

"Definitely not," I said firmly. "I can't tell by looking at it what the effect that curse could have on you."

"Fine," grumbled Pike. "Just give me a few minutes and I'll get right back to you."

The call ended and I looked over at Conall. "On the plus side, whoever is trying to kill me is still in town."

Conall frowned at my attempt to find a silver lining. "This just seems so crude and dramatic. It's like they're making a statement, but I don't understand who the audience is supposed to be."

"Maybe the town," I suggested. "If there are any other cursebreakers out there, it's a way of warning people not to provide sanctuary. I got a lot of support at the town meeting. That can't be good for a group that's desperate to kill me."

Conall gathered me in his arms and pulled me to the

center of the house. "If all the exit points are wired we need to stay as far away from them as possible."

From what Pike had shown me, I wasn't sure that was going to make any difference.

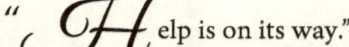

19

"*H*elp is on its way."

It took a few seconds before I heard the sirens that Conall's superior werewolf hearing had already heard.

Conall's phone rang and he put it on speaker.

"So, Pike is telling me we can't touch this bomb."

I couldn't explain how grateful I was to hear Karl's voice. Despite how fond I was of Pike, he didn't have the same calm, authoritative way about him that Deputy Iversen carried at all times.

"Correct," the sheriff replied. "Sadie has seen that it is covered in a curse. We have no idea how it is going to affect whoever touches it. It can't be disarmed until she gets rid of that curse."

"And you've tried all the other exits?"

"Yes," confirmed Conall. "We can't even break the windows."

I could see Karl's frown on the screen. "Doesn't that seem weird?" he finally asked. "I would have thought the whole reason for this device would be to blow you up as you opened the door. It kind of defeats the purpose if you can't leave the house."

"You're working with the same information we've got," Conall said. "I really don't have anything else to add."

"Okay," Karl squared his shoulders. "You two hold tight. We're going to see if there are any other devices, or if there is another way to get you out of the house."

To say that Conall wasn't thrilled with that plan was an understatement. He wasn't exactly the kind of person who dealt well with sitting and waiting. As we heard the sounds of deputies traipsing around the house I watched as an agitated Conall paced across the floor.

"If I went into berserker mode, I may be able to break that window," he muttered.

"Have you ever been able to call down the berserker without being really angry?" I was curious. It wasn't exactly something we talked about. It was the side of him that came out in times of extreme stress. As annoying as this situation was, it lacked the immediate danger that we'd had before.

"No," Conall replied. "I've never tested it."

"Unless it's absolutely necessary, I don't know whether right now is a great time to start." I knew how much he hated being trapped, but we had to be smart before we made a bad situation that much worse.

My phone rang and I answered it. I was relieved when Flora's face filled the screen.

"Are you okay?" she asked urgently.

"We're fine," I assured her. "As long as we don't leave the house, we seem to be okay."

"I'm outside. Tell me what you need me to do."

"I need you to make sure nobody attempts to touch the bomb. It has a curse all over it and I have no idea what it would do to the person who tried to disarm it. I need to get to it first."

She nodded. "I can do that."

"I also need you to check the grounds for any magical traps," I said. "I have no idea why we can't leave the house. It just seems weird to put a bomb on my door and then trap me in the house so I can't set it off."

"That does seem strange," she replied.

Conall tapped me on the shoulder and indicated he had something to tell me. "I've got to go, Flora. Let me know if you find anything."

"What's up?" I asked as I ended the call.

"Pike and Iversen have finished their sweep of the house," Conall replied. "We both need to hear what they have to say."

I leaned against Conall as we listened intently to the men trying to save us.

"Each of the three doors to the house have a bomb attached to them," Iversen said. "The bombs are very basic in design. They are triggered to go off when you open the door or, failing that, there is a timer on each of them."

"When's the timer due to go off?" Conall asked, his tone subdued.

"We have fifteen minutes," Iversen replied grimly.

That didn't sound like a lot of time.

"How big should the explosion be?" Conall asked. "Is there anywhere in this house that might keep us safe?"

Pike shook his head. "The explosion will be a good enough size that it will take down a significant portion of the house. The second one explosion goes, the shockwave will most likely trigger the other two."

"I need options," Conall barked.

"Already way ahead of you, Sheriff," Pike replied.

"We're not going with your plan," Iversen gritted out. "Despite how annoying you are, I'm not interested in breaking in a new partner."

The fact that it was Pike's plan caused a sinking feeling in the pit of my stomach.

"Lay it out," I could tell that Conall was a little wary about any plan that Pike had a hand in.

"It's simple really." Pike smiled and it disturbed me that he was showing no fear whatsoever. "The bomb is basic. It's like somebody got the plans off the internet. And not good plans like you can find on the Dark Web. I'm talking the plans that you find in the equivalent of a kiddie pool."

Considering how little time we had, Pike didn't seem to be particularly rushed. Conall must have agreed.

"Can we move this along, please," he demanded.

"Fine," Pike drawled. "I cut the wires between the explosive and the detonator. Iversen here has a crowbar and a sledgehammer to get the door open using brute force. If it's being held by something magical, we've got the coven leader as backup to break whatever spell is doing this."

"No, no, no." There was no way he could do this. "The second you touch this thing the curse will hit you. It could kill you or it could send you mad. I don't know."

Pike continued as if I hadn't spoken. "Once the door is opened, Sadie comes out and breaks the curse, and we all go for a well-deserved beer."

Conall was watching me as I vigorously shook my head. "Do we have any other options?"

"I really wish we did," Iversen replied. "We just don't have time for anything else. All three of these bombs need to have the curse removed and be deactivated within the next ten minutes."

"We're wasting time," Pike grumbled. "We're doing this." He reached over and ended the call.

"No!" I screamed. I raced to the front door and started yelling through it. "Don't you dare do this."

Conall pulled me back from the door. "He's not going to

listen to anything either of us has to say," he murmured as I struggled in his arms.

"He can't die for me," I cried.

"I think you're the one person he likes enough that he would be willing to die for."

For a second there was silence and then I heard an inhuman wail of unimaginable pain.

"Stand back!" Karl bellowed and I waited for the splintering of the door. I think it surprised us all when it simply sprang open.

I lunged from Conall's arms and ignored his shouted warning as I ran outside. I found Pike writhing on the ground, his body covered in tendrils, Flora standing to the side, knowing that she couldn't get near him but desperate to help.

I dropped to my knees beside Pike and ignored his flailing limbs as I swept my hands over his body, destroying as many of the tendrils as I could as quickly as I could. I kept going, even when one of his fists caught me a glancing blow on my cheek. Once I'd destroyed all of the tendrils I headed towards the cause of the curse. The bomb was still attached to the side of the house with wires hanging haphazardly from it. It looked like Pike had not been delicate about the operation. He had simply grabbed the wires and yanked. I put my hands on both sides of the bomb and squeezed. I watched in satisfaction as the whole thing crumbled into dust. I never understood how I was able to destroy things while breaking a curse that I would never have the strength to do at any other time.

I felt my arm being grabbed. "You have six minutes for the other two," Karl snarled as he pulled me up from my knees. "We have to do this now." I raced with him around the back of the house and found the second explosive. Following

Pike's example, I yanked the wires and then crushed the bomb.

By the time we made it up to the deck I had no idea how much time we had left. I just stepped up to the bomb and destroyed it. I slumped to the ground. So much for me trying to save my soul by avoiding curses completely. I grimaced at the oily feeling I couldn't seem to brush off from my hand.

I headed down the steps from the deck and found Flora with Pike. From the way her lips were moving I could see that she was chanting spells in an attempt to help ease his suffering. The curse that had been attached to the bombs was supposed to cause instant and unrelenting pain. When I'd been destroying the tendrils that had been writhing across him, I could see that the curse had set his body on fire. Not just the skin. The curse had reached inside him and it had felt like his organs were boiling. Whoever had put this curse in place took a kind of enjoyment in human suffering that horrified me.

I dropped to my knees next to Pike and took his other hand. The fact that he was still whimpering in pain gave me some small idea of what he had gone though. The Deputy Beastpike I knew would never whimper in his life. I felt a tear drop from my eye and land on him.

Flora reached over to me. "He's going to be alright," she said. "You saved him."

"He wouldn't have had to be saved if it wasn't for me."

That's what hurt the most. The bombing was never going to hit just me. Anyone who had been watching me knew that I always had someone with me, whether it was Conall, Pike, Tilda or Flora. One of them was always going to be in the line of fire. All because of me.

"Don't."

I almost missed Flora's warning, her voice was so low.

"Don't what?" I asked, as I tried to suppress the hollow feeling inside me.

"This was not your fault."

I didn't even bother to reply. Pretty words did not help me right now. What was real was the fact that someone who cared about me in his own way had gone through the most agonizing pain I could imagine, all to protect me.

By the time the paramedics finally got to us I was beside myself. Even though I'd broken the curse, it took time for the effects to resolve themselves. I just hoped I got to him quickly enough to ensure that there wasn't going to be any permanent damage.

"I'm going with him to the clinic," I announced as Pike was being loaded into the ambulance, almost daring Conall to argue. He must have seen something in my eyes because he nodded his head at Karl to follow me. I pulled myself up into the back of the ambulance.

"You can't be in here," the paramedic argued. "Only medical personnel can be back here."

Just my luck to come up against a rule follower.

"He has been cursed," I bit out and noticed that her eyes widened. "If something weird happens with that curse on the trip to the clinic, you're going to be thrilled that I'm hitching a ride." I found a spare seat and parked myself in it.

Fortunately for me, the paramedic was also a pragmatist, and Pike's moans convinced her that this was not the moment to argue the point. She pulled shut the doors and busied herself taking care of Pike's vitals. She didn't see the slight smile on Pike's face. I had a feeling not all of those moans were involuntary. I should have known that even while in agonizing pain, he would still have my back.

20

*W*ords could not begin to describe how grateful I was to see Dr Collias when we reached the clinic. As the paramedics unloaded Pike, he gestured for me to start talking.

"There was a bomb on my house. It also had a curse on it so anyone who tried to disarm it would be incapacitated. I was trapped in the house so was not able to get to the bomb before it could be disarmed."

"And Pike being Pike decided to just disarm it and damn the consequences," Collias said.

"There were time constraints," I replied.

"Of course, there were." Collias shook his head. "What were the effects of the curse?"

"Pain," I said simply. "Agonizing, unrelenting pain. It was designed to make him feel like he was burning from the inside out. I've broken the curse, but I don't know if I was quick enough to prevent any lasting effects."

Collias shook his head. "No offense, but I missed the time when curses were the stuff of legends."

"They were never just the stuff of legends," I pointed out

bitterly. "They were just much better ignored when there wasn't anything that could be done about them."

"I stand corrected." Collias frowned. "Is that a bruise on your face?"

"It's nothing." I dropped my head forward. "I'll deal with it after you tell me Pike is okay."

"Understood." He turned away and followed the paramedics.

One of the few benefits of the amount of time I had spent in the clinic since arriving in Walker Bay was that I knew where they stored certain items. It wasn't long before I was in the waiting room with an ice pack against my face. A large ogre squatted down in front of me and tipped up my head.

"That doesn't look good."

I flinched away from him. "It's nothing."

I could see he didn't believe me, but compared to what Pike had gone through, I could have a fractured skull and it wouldn't even begin to rate.

Karl stood up and sat down next to me, the chair groaning at his weight. "How's he going?"

"I don't know," I replied. "They just took him in. I'm pretty sure he was conscious in the ambulance, but the pain meant he wasn't communicative." I rubbed my hands across my eyes, trying to keep the tears that were threatening to fall from overwhelming me.

Karl leaned back and put a hand on my shoulder. "He cares about you very much. He might act like nothing affects him but when someone earns his loyalty, it's for life. He's that way with the sheriff and he's included you in his circle."

That was sweet but it didn't help. "There had to be a better way to do this."

"There probably was," Karl agreed. "But we had ten minutes. What else could we do in ten minutes? Second guessing ourselves now is not going to help the situation."

I knew he was making sense, but I was wallowing too deeply in my own self-pity to listen. I looked up at the clattering of hooves coming down the hallway.

"I'm guardedly optimistic," announced the doctor as he entered the room.

"What kind of bedside manner is that?" barked Karl. "How about telling us that he's fine."

Collias crossed his arms and gave Karl the look that echoed generations of warrior centaurs. "Because he's not fine. He's very far from fine. Whoever cast that curse has a sadistic streak in them a mile long. The fact he went through that much pain without his heart giving out is a miracle beyond belief."

I always found it concerning when doctors talked about miracles. I preferred a doctor who was willing to tell me in minute detail the efforts they went to when saving a life, and how much they should be congratulated for their god-like brilliance.

"I want to stay with him," I announced.

There was still a small part of me that was concerned this curse had a sting in the tail that I hadn't seen in my rush to disarm the bombs. I'd had a glimpse into the mind of the person who cast it and it hadn't been pretty. They weren't just out to kill a cursebreaker. They were going to enjoy the destruction that they caused on the way to their ultimate goal.

Collias arched an eyebrow. "Do you think that is necessary?"

I held his gaze. "I don't know, but I'd rather be there in case it becomes necessary."

"Very well." I was relieved that he wasn't going to argue with me.

He led me to Pike's room and my heart sank. The one thing I'd always noticed about Pike was how vibrant he was.

He could never be still, and his face was always so expressive, which was amazing when you consider how much of it was covered by his beard. All of that was gone. He was pale and the lines in his face had deepened to crevices. I sat down beside his bed and gathered his hand in mine.

"You need to wake up," I demanded. "I'm really mad at you for doing something so reckless, so I need you to wake up so that I can yell at you and then you can tell me that you had everything under control, and you can laugh at me for being so scared."

Collias watched as I threatened his patient. "He'll wake up soon. We just put him to sleep temporarily so his body can heal."

He left me with my fallen protector and I settled in and watched over him for a change.

IT WASN'T long before the sheriff and Flora joined me.

"How is he?" Conall asked as he pulled up a chair next to me and started rubbing his hand over my back as if trying to release some of the tension that he could see.

"In pain," I answered. The past hour had been devastating to watch as Pike had twitched and moaned in his sleep. "Dr Collias said he just needs some time to heal. I feel bad because I want him to wake up so I know that he's okay."

Conall smiled at my impatience. "If there is one thing I know about Pike, it is that he will do things in his own sweet time. Trying to make him do anything is the best incentive for him to do the complete opposite."

My lips pulled into a small smile. That didn't surprise me at all.

"Did you find anything at the house?"

Conall slumped in his chair. "Just what we saw. Three

devices, all separate, connected to the three doors. The devices were crude as if someone with very little knowledge had put them together. We're probably lucky that they didn't go off accidentally. Whoever did this did not have any skills."

"Maybe not as bomb makers, but they knew what they were doing when it came to curses," I said, the bitterness choking me as my eyes swung back to Pike. "That curse was vicious, and it was aimed to kill whoever tried to disarm those bombs."

Conall gripped my shoulder. "Then we're lucky it was Pike. He's too stubborn to let something like that take him out."

I certainly hoped so.

"Why weren't we able to get out of the house?" I still hadn't worked out why that had happened. It didn't seem to fit with the rest of the attack.

"Yeah," drawled Conall. "Flora's got an interesting theory on that one."

I looked over at Flora and waited expectantly.

"I believe that your house recognized the threat and protected you in the only way it could."

I waited for the punchline. "You are kidding, aren't you?"

Flora shook her head. It took me a minute before the full extent of what she was saying to me sank in. I looked over at Conall hoping he'd provide some sanity.

"Don't look at me. I've lived in the paranormal world my whole life and I've never heard of anything like this."

"You're telling me my house is alive and that it made the decision to protect us from the bombs that had been attached to it?" I wanted to be entirely sure that I didn't misunderstand what was being said here.

"Not alive like you would think," Flora clarified. "Throughout history there have been occasions when an object has been so mired in magic that it takes on certain abilities that would give the appearance of some form of awareness." She stopped for a moment as if trying to think of an appropriate analogy. "Bacteria doesn't have sentience, but it can react to external stimuli. Your house did the same thing."

"You're saying my house is some form of bacteria?" The more Flora spoke, the worse the situation became.

"I'm saying it takes on similar attributes. Bacteria can adapt to situations and mutate. Your house reacted to a threat it did not understand so it locked down to protect you."

"If it was trying to protect us why did it block the windows?" Conall asked. "We couldn't even break them to get out. That would have been the ideal solution to the problem."

Flora looked pained. "It isn't using any sense of reason. It's acting on instinct. Something bad is outside so lock down everything."

"And when Pike disarmed the bomb on the front door it felt one of the threats being neutralized so the door swung open to let us out," I said as I started following Flora's reasoning. "That's insane. How could that happen?"

"I would think that decades of being under a curse is enough to infuse anything with a sense of magic," Flora suggested. "When you broke the curse, you would have also used a massive amount of power to destroy it. Between those two strong opposing forces, it's not surprising that something has happened to that house. I think we should consider ourselves lucky that the building came out of that mess with some protective instincts rather than an insatiable desire for human blood."

That was a lovely thought.

"Protection or self-preservation?" Conall queried. "If any of those bombs had gone off, the house would be destroyed. I wouldn't be so quick to attribute human emotions to a building, regardless of what kind of magic has run through it. I also wouldn't be so quick to dismiss the potential for evil."

"No," I said firmly. "That house isn't evil. It's my home and it has never made me feel unsafe." I wasn't sure why I was so certain. I just was.

"Do you lot ever stop talking?"

"Pike!" I leaned over and had to stop myself from squeezing the poor deputy.

Pike tried to give us his trademark frown, but it collapsed into a pained grimace.

"What do you need?" I asked.

"The ability to make better choices," he replied.

I rolled my eyes. "We know that would be wasted on you because you'd just ignore it anyway. Do you need some more pain relief? I can get the doctor."

Pike put his hand over mine. "It wasn't your fault. I made the choice and I was willing to accept the consequences of that choice."

I took a deep breath as I put my other hand over his. "I could feel what you went through. Nobody should go through that kind of pain."

Pike gave a small grin. "Oh, I've got a list of people who I wouldn't mind going through it."

Of course he did. I gave him an answering smile before dipping my head and giving him a kiss on the forehead. "Thank you. I wasn't sure how we were going to get out of that one."

"It's good to see our patient is feeling better."

I was surprised I hadn't heard Dr Collias approach the room. I'd never thought of centaurs as being stealthy.

"What makes you think I'm feeling better?"

"You're conscious," Collias replied. "Of all the outcomes available to us today, I'm thinking that is the best one."

"I don't feel particularly lucky," he grumbled.

"Trust me," Collias replied. "You weren't supposed to survive that curse. The only reason you did is because Sadie got to you so quickly. She saved your life."

I could tell from the expression on Pike's face that he wasn't particularly fond of that turn of events.

"After he saved ours," I injected, trying to smooth the deputy's ruffled feathers.

"I think he needs some rest," Collias announced.

I glanced at Pike and could see the toll the day had taken. I'd wait until he was a bit stronger before I yelled at him and extracted a promise that he would never risk himself like that again. Not too strong, though. Otherwise I wouldn't have a fighting chance of getting my point across.

Conall stepped up beside me and I could feel his hand placed at the small of my back. I nodded and tried very hard to keep a smile on my face. It would be a long time before I could let go of the guilt for the pain he had gone through.

"I'll be back soon," I promised.

Pike gave a weak wave of his hand. "Take your time."

21

*A*s we stepped into the waiting area I stopped short at the sight before me. Of all the people I would have expected to see, my newly found stepsiblings and cousins wouldn't have come anywhere close to the top of the list. Tilda I was expecting, and there she was, looking exceedingly uncomfortable surrounded by Harstones. She looked up at me with relief in her eyes. There was also something else in her expression that I couldn't quite read.

"Is Pike okay?"

"He's fine," I replied, still trying to get my head around what I was seeing. "Collias is keeping him in until he's sure that there's no lasting damage."

Tilda stood up from the chair and stepped forward as if to distance herself from the rest of the people in the room. "That's good." She glanced at the sheriff standing beside me, tension radiating from him, and I could see her holding in a sigh.

She leaned forward to give me a hug. "I have no idea why these people are here," she whispered into my ear.

That made two of us and I couldn't say it made me very comfortable.

One of the men cleared their throat and I wracked my brain to work out which one it was. The dinner with the Harstones had been a blur of high stress and judgement. Taking in names had not been my highest priority.

"The family is concerned for your safety," he announced.

He kept his eyes on me, not acknowledging the man standing behind me whose professed sole purpose in life was to keep me safe. I really did not want to deal with this now.

"I don't think you need to," I said through gritted teeth. For a day that had started out with such promise, it had gone downhill fast.

The man whose name I wish I could remember chose his words carefully. "We have access to people who can keep you safe. You will be in protective custody until the authorities can track down whoever is doing this."

Some might call that offer the sign of a caring family. Others might call it an attempt by the predators to separate me from the protection of my herd. From the way Conall and Tilda were standing, I was pretty sure I knew which option they believed.

"Why are you the one offering this?" I asked. If anybody was going to try to bully me into protective custody, I would have thought it would be Collette.

"He's your brother," one of the women inserted herself into the conversation. "That means he wants to protect you."

Aah, that meant I was talking to Tade Blackwood. The son of the woman who had made the questionable decision to marry the man I had always considered the worst example of his gender. Not exactly what I would call the basis for a loving sibling relationship.

I took a closer look at the group and cast my mind back to the dinner at the manor. It hadn't been Tade's sister who believed in the happily ever after version of our family. It had been Malin, one of my triplet cousins, and if I wasn't mistaken she seemed to have an affection for my stepbrother. From the looks of him, he didn't have a clue. I shook my head. How did I walk into this situation?

"Why are you here?" I asked as I reached the end of my admittedly limited patience. "I don't know you. If we were all being honest for just five minutes we would admit that I'm not part of this family. Not really."

If my honesty surprised them, they didn't show it.

"Regardless of our feelings about the situation, you're a Harstone. We don't allow Harstones to be targets. Not now. Not ever."

That would be Rebecca, the second of my female cousins. It looked like she was not a fan of my appearance in the Harstone family tree. I could respect that. At least she was being honest. Taking a recap, I had Tade who seemed to want me to be safe. There was Malin who just wanted whatever Tade wanted. Rebecca couldn't care less about me, but she did care something about the Harstone name. Elijah Harstone and Lorelei Blackwood had remained silent, but I could feel them watching me, assessing me as if they weren't entirely sure about me and wanted further information before coming to a decision.

"We need to take this somewhere else." It seemed that Elijah had decided to join the conversation. "Somewhere private."

"That's not going to happen," growled Conall. "If you want to talk to Sadie, it is going to be in a public space with plenty of witnesses."

I could tell that Elijah wanted to say something to Conall. I stepped closer to him and hoped my family got the message. My Destined Beloved came first in all things. Attacking him was off-limits.

Tade scrubbed his hand through his hair. "We are not the ones trying to hurt you," he growled. "We're the ones trying to keep you safe."

"I don't know that," I replied honestly. "I don't know you and the fact that I've had someone try to murder me since you arrived in town doesn't really inspire confidence in our familial bond."

"We could go to the diner."

Lorelei's suggestion came from left field.

"You think that's private enough for what you want to say?" I asked.

"Of course not," she replied, "but if we want to talk to you, we'll only be able to do it in public. We can block anyone hearing and maybe we can build some trust."

It just went to show that you had to watch the quiet ones. They had the tendency to be the real thinkers in the group. I glanced up at Conall. As far as my security went, I was more than willing to accede to his wishes. Two murder attempts had knocked the stubborn independence out of me. I could be as pig-headed as I wanted when I was the only one getting hurt. Now that people I cared about were in the firing line, I was going to listen to Conall's advice as if he knew everything.

"Not the worst idea I've heard today," he commented. "We'll meet you there in fifteen minutes."

"Does anybody else think this is weird?" Tilda asked once we were settled in the sheriff's truck. It seemed she had decided that a meeting of the current generation of the Harstone clan was not something she wanted to miss. "And not normal Walker Bay weird. I'm talking horror movie weird."

"You mean you don't believe that the family is willing to welcome me with open arms?"

"I'd say that's as likely as Aidan Tolan welcoming you as his new daughter."

I winced at the analogy. I hadn't thought it was that bad.

"I'm surprised you were willing to meet with them," I said to Conall. "I figured that you would be a lot more reticent about the idea of me being anywhere near them."

"You know what they say about keeping your enemies close?" he drawled. "I think this might be a good chance for us to get some intel."

"You think they are the enemy?"

"They're Harstones," he replied. "I will be shocked if they aren't the enemy."

22

J glanced around the diner and couldn't help the wry smile pulling at my lips. It seemed that pretty much every deputy in Walker Bay had decided to get something to eat at that precise moment.

"Not taking any chances," Conall whispered in my ear. I thought he'd agreed to this potential disaster a little too quickly.

The rest of the Harstone clan had taken over a few tables and put them together.

I straightened my shoulders. "Let's do this."

We headed towards the back of the diner and I noticed that Tilda had taken the lead and Conall was at my back, both of them shielding me. I really hated the fact they felt the need to do that.

When we reached the tables, Elijah stood up, a frown on his face. "This is a Harstone family meeting," he said. "I accept we can't separate you from the berserker, but what is she doing here?" he asked as he gestured towards Tilda.

Honestly, I wasn't really sure why Tilda had decided to join us, but I wasn't sending her away.

"She's with me," I said firmly. Tilda knew more about the Harstones than I did. If anyone was going to be able to give me a rundown on how this meeting meshed with witch politics it would be her. "If she's not welcome, I'm leaving."

The family glanced at each other and Elijah gave a resigned nod.

"Also, stop calling Conall 'the berserker'. He's the sheriff in Walker Bay. Show him the respect he deserves."

That got me an even tighter nod. I sat down and looked around. This was my family and I had absolutely nothing in common with these people. When I'd been a kid and had a vague fantasy about meeting family, I had always thought that I would feel some familial tie with them. I felt nothing. I couldn't see any physical similarities between me and my cousins. If I hadn't had the DNA test and Flora's insistence that I was a Harstone, I would be thinking that a terrible mistake had been made. I pulled out my privacy spell from my pocket and placed it in the middle of the table. If we were going to do this, we'd better get started.

"What is that?"

I had thought that my stepsister was shy and overlooked by the strong personalities around her. I was wrong, she just needed to see something that rocked her understanding of the world.

"It's my privacy spell," I explained.

"It's a troll doll," she replied with just a tinge of contempt in her voice. I was impressed that she'd managed to verbally contain what was reflected on the faces of the rest of her family.

"It was my first spell and I haven't had a chance to replace it with something more appropriate." I didn't think they needed to know that my troll doll was my only real successful spell. It was a lesson for the ages. Just because you are talented in one area didn't necessarily translate to other areas of your life. I knew some singers who thought they could act who needed to remember that life lesson.

"It's the strongest privacy spell I've ever seen," Tilda interjected. "It doesn't matter what it looks like. Not even a magister can get through it."

Considering the number of times Tilda had made fun of my troll doll, I was touched by her defense of it. I was surprised when Malin started talking. She'd seemed to be the most non-confrontational of the group.

"We are concerned that the danger you are in is going to overwhelm Walker Bay," she said. "The Conclave can protect you."

I cocked my head to the side. "Are you entirely sure about that? Last time I checked, being a cursebreaker put me on the Conclave Most Wanted list, and nothing that has happened in the last few weeks has done anything to convince me otherwise."

"We have a guarantee from the Conclave that you will be safe, as long as you meet with them," Malin said.

That was an interesting way to phrase the offer. If I was a suspicious person I would consider it a threat.

"Has the law been repealed?" I asked.

"What do you mean?" Rebecca answered. It was interesting to see how the other two female members of this generation of Harstones worked together, diverting attention from each other in a way that kept you uncertain.

"It's a pretty simple question. Has the law that sentences cursebreakers to death been repealed or is it still able to be enacted?"

Rebecca looked helplessly at the others. "It's an old law. It would take time to remove. It doesn't mean that it will be used."

I gave her a small smile as I tried to keep the cynicism from showing. "As long as it is still a law, somebody may be tempted to use it against me. I can't take that chance with my life or the lives of the people I care about." Because I knew that if the Conclave came after me they would have to go through Conall. That was a risk I would never be willing to take.

"The Conclave wants to understand what happened with Liam Rigby," Tade said.

My head was beginning to hurt with the fact that everybody was contributing to this conversation and the topics were jumping around. It made it hard to get a read on anybody. I wondered if they were doing it on purpose. I felt Tilda stiffen beside me. We had been working very hard at not mentioning his name for the last couple of weeks.

"Bringing up the magister who tore through this town does not increase the likelihood of me accepting the Conclave's proposal. People died because of him, including one he murdered in his hospital bed."

"Liam Rigby was well-known and well-liked," Elijah said, showing a breathtaking ability to ignore the evidence in front of him. "The notion that he was killed while investigating a cursebreaker has caused some disquiet in the Conclave. You must understand that your existence and your ability to kill a magister is causing some concern."

"Rigby wasn't killed," Conall announced to my surprise. I'd thought we were keeping any information about the magister on a need to know basis. I didn't understand why he now thought the Harstones needed to know.

"We saw the video." Rebecca's quiet voice dropped in the middle of the conversation and I could feel myself tense. I'd known that the video of my confrontation with Liam Rigby had been streaming somewhere. I just hadn't known how far it had gone.

"He was hurt," Conall said, "but a mercy was shown to him that he didn't deserve. He survived the encounter."

In moments like this I could see the warrior in the sheriff. I knew that he had accepted my decision to spare Liam's life, but I had a feeling he wasn't happy with it.

"Then where is he?" asked Tade. "He should be brought before the Conclave to face justice for his actions."

I wasn't entirely sure that the Conclave's version of justice for a magister would match mine.

"Liam Rigby is currently being held pending charges," Conall replied smoothly. "The Conclave will have to wait to exercise jurisdiction."

I could see that nobody at the table was happy with that answer.

"Where is he?" Tade leaned forward, his eyes flashing. "This is witch business. I'm getting a little tired of this town dictating to us."

I could feel the tension in the room increase. Despite not being able to hear what was happening at our table, there was no mistaking the body language.

"Let's listen to what the sheriff has to say," Elijah drawled, his relaxed expression not fooling anybody.

Both Lorelei and Malin had put a soothing hand on each of Tade's arms as if trying to pull him back from a confrontation that he had little hope of winning. It was interesting to note that all conversation about the Harstones protecting me had gone out the window. It looked like we were now getting to the real reason they had approached me.

"Liam Rigby committed murder in this town." The sheriff's voice hardened. "That murder was of a werewolf which takes this crime out of Conclave jurisdiction. He also cast curses on several people in Walker Bay. He used his powers against various races. The Conclave could only conceivably claim jurisdiction if all his crimes had been against witches. They weren't which means his crimes come under Assembly jurisdiction." He leaned forward. "I know you will report this entire conversation to Collette so let me be completely clear. Liam Rigby will feel the full force of the law. His position as magister will not give him special treatment. The Conclave needs to understand that the rest of the world is not theirs for the taking."

He stood up and Tilda and I followed. "I have no idea why you chose to approach us like this, but you need to understand that Walker Bay is not a town where you can walk in and take over. If that is the Conclave's plan, I can guarantee that it is going to get bloody."

I swiped my troll doll from the table and followed Conall out, grateful that the deputies in the diner were watching our backs. It was only when we settled in the sheriff's truck that I broke the silence.

"That went well, if by well you mean declaring war on the Conclave."

Conall looked over at me, his expression grim. "We're already at war. I was just letting them know that we knew it."

23

*W*hat the hell is that?"

After we dropped Tilda off at home we headed for my house. For the first time I felt a little nervous at the prospect of staying there. It wasn't every day that someone floated the idea that your house may be coming alive. I still wasn't sure how I felt about that. My concern wasn't helped by the shimmering that now encompassed the entire house.

Usually Conall pulled up near the front door. This time he kept well back. As he parked the truck his phone rang so he was distracted when I hopped out to take a closer look at whatever this was.

"Your aunt does not do things halfway, does she?"

I should have been more surprised to see Julian standing to the side of the house, but this had been one of those days.

"What do you mean?" I asked. This looked an awful lot like the shield that Liam Rigby had used to protect himself when he'd kidnapped Tilda.

"I believe it's a protection shield," he replied, confirming my suspicions as he stepped closer to me. "I've just never seen anybody who was strong enough to create one that covered an entire building before."

I looked over at Conall who was keeping an eye on us as he talked on the phone. I could tell that whatever he was being told was not lessening the tension that seemed to surround him these days.

"I understand why she did it," Julian said, his hands tucked in his pockets as if trying to look less threatening. "She loves you and wants to protect you anyway she can."

I appreciated the sentiment, but even with my limited knowledge of magic, I knew that whatever she did here must have cost her dearly.

"We need to go in."

I'd been so distracted by the enormity of what Flora had done that I hadn't realized that Conall had moved up next to me.

"How do we get in?" I asked.

"We walk in like any other day," Conall said, an encouraging smile playing on his lips. I knew he was trying to appear calm, but I could see the tension in the lines around his eyes. Whatever that conversation on the phone had been, it was causing him stress. "The shield won't hurt us."

I hoped he was right. The last time I'd faced one of these shields, I'd managed to use my cursebreaker power to break through it. Of course, that power had come from a place deep inside me where there had been other people's anger and brutality. I really didn't want to have to do that again.

Conall took my hand and pulled me behind him through the shield. The feeling as I passed through was like a slight pins and needles sensation on my skin. I barely felt it at all. I wish I could say the same about Julian who tried to follow us. I jerked back at the loud thump as Julian flew through the air and landed heavily on the ground.

"You're not on the list, Bernauer," the sheriff said coldly.

I watched as Julian picked himself off the ground and wiped some of the dirt off his pants. He didn't say a word, just turned and walked back to his house.

"What is this?" I asked as I put my hand out to touch the light.

"It's a magic far beyond anything I've ever seen," Conall said. "Every time I believe I have a handle on how powerful Flora is, she shows me that I have no idea."

"Is she okay?" I had a feeling she wasn't. If Flora was still okay she would have been here, explaining what she had done.

"She did what she had to do to protect you," Conall said, the gentle tone warring with the command in his voice. "We have to accept her choice."

"Where is she?" If Conall Tolan thought for one moment that I was going to let him stop me from seeing my only family member—the only family I cared about—he was going to learn a whole new lesson in what it meant to be in a relationship with me.

Conall raised his hands as if to head off the explosion heading his way. "What she did here was beyond what any one witch should have been able to do. By rights she should have called in the coven, but she knew that some of them have strong opinions on your cursebreaker abilities. She didn't want those members tainting the strength of the shield. Instead she did it on her own.

"Where is she?" I didn't intend to ask a third time.

Conall dropped his head. "She's at her home with Maude watching over her. She's unconscious and will be for some time. This shield took the last of her strength."

I started to head for my car. "I'm going to see her. She needs to be here where I can take care of her. I'll take her to the clinic so Collias can have a look at her first."

Conall grabbed me and pulled me into his arms. "She needs to rest and you need to honor the sacrifice she made. She turned this house into a safe place for you. How do you think you would have been able to sleep tonight, knowing that somebody could blow us up? She isn't dead and she isn't in any danger of dying. She is simply rebuilding her strength after she over-extended herself. Her home is the best place for her to do that. Let her heal where she doesn't feel like a burden on you."

I sagged against him. "She could never be a burden. I should be there for her."

"And she should let you be there for her, but she's very stubborn, not unlike somebody else I know. Some would say it's a family trait."

Trust me, it wasn't only the Harstone side where I got that stubbornness.

"Does she need anything? Can I pack some things for her?" I asked, unwilling to give up completely.

"Maude said that she had everything taken care of. Flora just needs to rest."

"This isn't right." Anger at the situation flowed through me.

"I know it isn't, sweetheart," he said as he stroked his hands down my arms. "But they're the cards we've been dealt."

I took a deep breath and tried to fight the tears I could feel building. "I can't keep living like this."

"I'll protect you," Conall vowed.

I had no doubt he would. My biggest fear wasn't that he wouldn't protect me. It was that I could lose him while he was protecting me. I was sick of waiting for the next move to happen.

"Why don't we use me as bait?"

Instead of the loud argument I was expecting, Conall

sighed. He stepped away and held out his hand. "We should discuss this inside," he said.

I took his hand and followed him through the door. Conall sat down on the couch and rather than letting me take a seat beside him, he pulled me down onto his lap and wrapped his arms around me.

"I know this is driving you crazy," he murmured. "I just don't want us to make a rash decision because we're scared." He pulled his head back and looked into my eyes. "Can you give me a bit more time before we start talking about deliberately putting you in danger."

"One more day," I said. "I will do what you want for one more day. I will not do anything to deliberately provoke a response from whoever is trying to kill me for one more day." I could tell this wasn't what Conall wanted to hear but we were playing too much of a defensive game.

"One more day," he repeated before brushing a sweet kiss against my lips. With surprising ease he lifted me off his lap and placed me on the couch before standing up.

"Where are you going?" I asked, a little surprised by the sudden movement.

"I have a day," he replied. "You are going to stay here while I go hunting."

The feral gleam in his eyes almost made me feel sorry for my attacker. Almost.

"Are you sending anyone over to babysit?"

Conall shook his head. "There's no need if you agree to stay here. Nobody can break through one of these shields," he said, his voice ringing with confidence.

"I did," I reminded him.

Conall's eyes darkened as he remembered the day we confronted Liam Rigby.

"Fortunately, there's only one of you in Walker Bay," he replied.

"We hope." I was really letting my pessimistic flag fly today. I wondered when I had got to this point.

"You'll be safe," Conall stated as if daring the universe to disagree.

I certainly hoped he was right.

24

*I*t's interesting that there are days when you are quite happy to stay at home and not even think of going somewhere else. That contentment seems to disappear when you no longer have a choice. Within minutes of Conall leaving I was climbing the walls, trying to figure out what I could do. Normally, I would have continued with my renovations on the house. However, there was now a part of me that was a little concerned with doing anything considering we were working with the theory that my house could in some way be sentient. I had no idea whether that meant I needed some form of consent before I continued with my projects. The fact that I was even considering issues like asking my house for permission was proof of how far down the rabbit hole I seemed to have fallen.

It wasn't long before I was reduced to flicking channels on the television, trying desperately to find something that could hold my interest. I was debating contacting Tilda to see if she could get some books from the coven library so I could feel like I was doing something useful when I heard a loud thump coming from the front of the house. It sounded familiar and I had a feeling that another person who was not on Flora's approved list was trying to gain access.

I opened the front door and wished I had pretended I wasn't at home.

"What are you doing here?"

The prone figure scrambled to his feet. "I want to speak to you, young lady."

I rolled my eyes at my father's attempt to actually be a father.

"You are not welcome in my home," I said simply. "I may not be able to avoid you, but I am definitely not going to go out of my way to be polite. Anyway, I didn't create this shield. I couldn't let you in even if I wanted to, which I don't."

Turning my back on my father I slammed the door as I retreated inside the house.

A moment later I heard him yell out. "Sadie, I need to talk to you. I'm not going away."

I opened the door again. "Really? 'Cause I was pretty sure that was your skill set."

Jasper flushed red and I couldn't tell whether it was from embarrassment or from anger. Frankly, I really didn't care.

He pulled himself upright. "I'm your father."

I looked him straight in the eye. "No, you're not. You are an unfortunate part of my existence, but you are definitely not my father."

"Is everything okay here?"

I should have known that Julian would not let this situation pass without his attention. I was horrified that we were playing out this drama in front of all my neighbors. I was not that person. Unfortunately, I didn't see a way around it. Conall would lose his mind if I left the safety of the shield, and I definitely wasn't going to find a way to get Jasper inside to continue this discussion.

"I wish to speak with my daughter." He pointed at Julian. "You have a relationship with her. Tell her to speak to me."

It was laughable to see the horrified expression on Julian's face. Even he could tell that Jasper was approaching me in the worst way possible.

"My relationship with Julian no longer exists," I said as calmly as I could. "I don't think you should be appealing for his help."

Jasper's eyes narrowed and I tensed at the calculating look in them. "I could tell you about your mother. I'm sure you want to hear about her, considering your loss."

I scowled at his attempt at emotional manipulation. "She told me all about the few hours you spent together," I said through gritted teeth. "She used it as an example of the worst kind of man that I could get involved with."

I could see Julian wince at the way that I was not going to give an inch.

"And yet you got involved with an engaged man," Jasper said slyly. "I'd suggest you didn't learn the lesson well enough."

Despite the fact that I was willing to lay many faults at the feet of Julian Bernauer, my sense of fairness wouldn't let this one pass.

"Even Julian did not run out on me while I was sleeping."

Julian shook his head. "You really don't think much of me, do you?"

"Trust me," I replied. "My opinion of you far exceeds what I think of that man."

"My understanding is that bar is set exceedingly low," Julian retorted.

I couldn't argue with that. "What do you want?" I snapped. "I don't believe that you're interested in having a happy family reunion. You've already got a new family. What do you need me for?"

Jasper stepped forward, still far enough away from the shield so he didn't go flying again but close enough to lower his voice a little. "You are my only natural child. Despite my best efforts, I have not been able to have another. Your power reflects on me. I think we could use it to benefit both our futures."

I couldn't stop the disgust that rolled through me. This man really was as despicable as I had been brought up to believe. I glanced over at Julian and could see the same thoughts going through his mind.

I was about to tell my dear father exactly what I thought of his proposal when a deputy's car rolled into the driveway. I breathed a sigh of relief when Deputy Iversen got out. The tension in him seemed to release when he saw that I was still safely behind the shield. His eyes narrowed when he spotted the two men I was talking to.

"Did you want to explain why we're getting calls from several houses in the street that there's a domestic disturbance happening here?"

I cringed in embarrassment. I usually liked to believe I was a good neighbor. No wild parties, no illicit drug deals and definitely no family drama in the front yard. I should not have been so surprised that it would be Walker Bay that changed all that.

Jasper straightened and gave the ogre a condescending look. "I am speaking to my daughter. I hardly believe that it is any of your concern."

Karl cocked his head. "When you bring a dispute out into the public domain it becomes the problem of the sheriff's department. Believe me when I say you do not want the sheriff to come down here and deal with you." He smiled, showing a set of pointy teeth. "I'm the nice one."

I snorted at that comment. I adored Karl and usually thought of him as a giant teddy bear. I was in the minority.

Jasper looked over at me and I could tell what he was thinking.

"You're not getting in here. I've thought your offer through and I not so regretfully decline." I crossed my arms and hoped he understood that any ambitions he had for using me or my abilities were not going to come to fruition.

It took him a few seconds but the words seemed to finally get through to him. Either that or he figured a strategic withdrawal now would serve him better in the future. I watched him walk away without another word and was surprised at the pang of regret that clawed its way through me. Despite my insistence that I didn't need a father, it seemed there was a part of me that would have liked things to have been different.

After Jasper left, Karl swung his head around to Julian. "Don't you have something better to do, Magister?"

Julian gave him a smile guaranteed to get his face punched in if circumstances had been different. "I was just being a concerned neighbor," he said. "I thought I'd do something a bit more proactive than just calling the police."

Karl pointed in the direction of Julian's house. "The problem has now been solved. You are no longer needed."

"He never was," I mumbled. "I had the situation in hand."

Karl grinned at me. "I had no doubt."

We watched as Julian headed back to his house.

"This is new," drawled Karl, his eyes drawn to the shimmering of the shield.

"My own little bubble," I replied. "Did you want to come inside? I'm sure Flora put an exemption in for you."

"Normally I'd agree with you," Karl said. "Unfortunately, I pulled her over for a broken taillight the other day. She hasn't been too thrilled with me since. I don't think my dignity could handle being flung through the air if I tried to enter and discovered the woman was still holding a grudge."

I shrugged and gave him my most innocent smile. "I'm sure she'd never do such a thing."

Karl snorted. "You know your aunt far better than that," he said. "It would be just like her to give me a dose of humility with a dash of respect for her power, and it would be just like you to facilitate her revenge."

I put my hand to my heart and fluttered my eyelashes in a way that I was sure looked more demented than coquettish. "I can't believe you think I am capable of such a heinous act."

Karl started laughing and I felt lighter than I had in days. "You keep believing that." He sobered. "I would suggest you stay behind that shield," he said. "Give the sheriff some time to work out who is behind this before you go off on your own." He looked down the road where Jasper had gone. "I don't know whether you want a relationship with your father, but you need to stay away from him for a little longer."

"Why?" I asked.

"We've been discovering things about him that are concerning."

"I'm shocked," I replied.

"Yeah." Karl rubbed the back of his neck. "Just...be careful who you trust."

↑

25

*N*ormally, I would have thought anybody having a one-sided conversation with their house was the first sign of a need for professional help. In my case, I figured it was the sanest thing I could do. If Flora was right and my house was developing some form of magical sentience, we were going to have to learn to co-exist. The last thing I needed was a home that could confine me if it felt I wasn't giving it the respect it was due.

So, while I cleaned my house, I talked. I told it about my perfectly normal life until I was kidnapped by a pair of elderly witches, desperate to save their friend. I had just got to the point where I was trying to explain the Destined Beloved prophecy and how I still had no idea how it could be a thing when everybody else in town thought I was an expert, when I heard something that felt entirely out of place in my new reality. A knock at the front door.

I moved as silently as I could and twitched the curtain at the front window.

"Oh, for goodness sake, Tilda, just come on in."

I was grateful that our theory of Flora providing exemptions for those closest to us had proven correct. I'm not sure how I would have felt if Tilda had gone flying through the air.

I watched her come through the door and frowned. "Why do you look like you're about to tell me my boyfriend got my grandmother pregnant?"

Tilda stopped, a startled expression on her face. "What?"

"When my mom was sick we watched a lot of daytime television together. That expression on your face is the same one I've seen on the faces of a significant number of guests on talk shows."

I had thought I'd get a laugh out of her, but she just looked pained. I sat down on the couch. Whatever she was about to tell me, I had a feeling I didn't want to be standing when I heard it.

"Just spit it out," I said. "I can take it, whatever it is." I really hoped that was true.

Tilda reached into her bag and pulled out a book. "I found a copy of this."

She passed it to me and I studied the cover. It was fairly nondescript and the title, 'There Is No Choice', gave me no idea about what it contained. From the expression on Tilda's face, I was willing to bet it wasn't anything good.

"What's this?"

Tilda sat opposite me. "That is a book that was released decades ago. It has been banned for nearly as long."

I frowned at that. I really wasn't fond of the idea of banning books. Unfortunately, it seemed that it was the favored method of the Conclave for dealing with unpopular ideas.

"It's basically a justification for the need to hunt down and kill cursebreakers. It's also an instruction manual on how to do that with a minimal amount of risk to yourself," Tilda continued.

In that case I was willing to make an exception. There was nothing like an immediate threat to your life to make you re-evaluate a lifetime of supposedly strongly held principles.

"Do I want to know where you found this book?"

I knew for sure that there was nothing like this in the coven library. When I first became librarian, I had searched for any book on cursebreakers that I could find. There had been very little information on the topic. Especially not an instruction manual on how to kill them. I was sure I'd remember that.

I watched as Tilda paced the room. I could tell that she was in one of those situations where she wanted to tell me something but she wasn't really sure how to say it. While waiting I flicked through the book and grimaced at some of the images. I could already tell that this was not going to be a pleasant read.

After several minutes Tilda flopped down on the seat opposite. "I found it at my grandmother's house a few days ago."

There was silence as I remembered the way Maude had reacted to the news that I was a cursebreaker. There had been real fear there which I hadn't understood. Although getting hold of a manual which detailed the best ways to kill me seemed to be a bit of an extreme over-reaction.

I looked over at Tilda and noted her miserable expression. My heart filled with sympathy. The fact that she'd found this book several days ago, and hadn't immediately reported it to Conall, gave me some indication of the struggle she had been going through. I had never questioned Tilda's friendship. For the first time that friendship was coming up against her loyalty to her family. The knowledge that she was putting her own grandmother in the sheriff's sights must have weighed on her.

"I wasn't going to tell you." Tilda's voice was low and I could barely make out what she was saying as she indicated the book in my hand. "She's my grandmother. I didn't want to think for one moment that she would be involved in something like this."

"She might not be," I said, desperate for a way to make this situation less painful. "You know that so many people have books that have been passed down from their ancestors. This could be one of them. She might not even know that she has a copy."

Tilda reached for the book and I gave it to her. She flicked through the pages and then passed it back, with the dedication page open.

I swallowed as I read out the words that were written by hand on the page. "To my dearest friend, Maude. Your support in our pursuit of a safer future has been invaluable. Your most ardent admirer, Isaac Sibley." I swallowed as I turned to the front of the book. Sure enough, the author's name was Isaac Sibley. All of a sudden my mouth went dry as a sudden thought struck me. "Maude's taking care of Flora. Is she safe?"

Tilda stood and put a calming hand on my shoulder. "I know Maude's loyalty to Flora is absolute. I would stake my life on it. She is safe. If you go down there, I'm not entirely sure whether you would be."

I leaned back on the couch and closed my eyes. "How did we get here?" Before this moment I would have never believed that I could possibly be in danger from Maude.

"I don't know." Tilda sat beside me and put her arm around my shoulders. "I can't believe she would have anything to do with trying to hurt you. That's not the woman I've known my entire life." She gestured toward the book. "I don't understand this. Nothing could make me understand this."

26

*"W*hat are you doing?"

I looked up in surprise. I hadn't been expecting Conall until late. I checked the time and grimaced. After Tilda had left, I had decided I should read Maude's book. I'd always thought that it was better to know what you were up against rather than embracing ignorance. I had quickly come to the conclusion that sometimes ignorance was best.

I waved the book I had been absorbed in for the last few hours as I slowly lost all faith in my fellow man. "I am reading a book written by a man who would happily slit my throat. From behind of course, because as Isaac Sibley says, you never kill a cursebreaker from the front. Always hit them when they can't possibly suspect you are coming."

Conall reached for the book and started reading the first page. I waited until I could see by the mounting tension in his face that he was understanding exactly what I had been doing with my time.

"Where did you get this?" he demanded.

"I need you to be calm and not react without thinking your next actions through very carefully."

"Sadie," he growled, impatiently.

"Tilda brought it over. She found it in Maude's house."

Conall sat down heavily on the couch, as if he was collapsing under the weight of what I had just said. "Please tell me that I have been working too hard and that I completely misheard what you just said."

"I wish I could."

"Any chance we're misunderstanding her having this book in her possession?"

Just as Tilda did, I opened the page to the dedication.

After Conall read it, he combed his fingers through his hair. "This is not good."

"What are you going to do?" I asked him, hoping for a measured response.

"I'm going to have to bring her in for questioning."

From the expression on his face I could tell that was not something that he was keen to do. I didn't blame him. In fact, I could put that last on my list of things I would want to do.

Conall stood up and held out a hand for me.

"Where are we going?" I asked as I slipped my hand in his.

"We are going to my office and I am going to get Karl to bring Maude in for questioning."

"Now?" I squeaked, thinking that this all seemed to be happening a bit quickly.

"I'm not leaving it until later," Conall grumbled. "This is the first concrete evidence that we have that someone in this town has a problem with you being a cursebreaker."

"But it's Maude."

Not only was she Tilda's grandmother. She was also number two in the coven. Well, number one with Flora being incapacitated.

I pulled back on Conall's hand. "We need to find someone to take care of Flora."

"Who do you trust?"

"Tilda," I said without hesitation. Tilda had proved herself time and again as being someone who had my back. The fact that she had brought me this book was final proof, if I needed it, which I hadn't. "I'll call Tilda and get her to sit with Flora." I hesitated. "Are you sure I can't bring her here?"

Conall sighed. "Flora's house is a place of power. I have a bad feeling we are going to need her very soon, so she needs to build her strength back up. If you bring her back here, the spell behind the shield will start draining her power again, and she's not yet strong enough to prevent it. We can't move her. Not yet."

"I don't like this," I muttered as I pulled out my phone.

"Neither do I," growled Conall.

WATCHING the sheriff as he interrogated a suspect was not a new experience for me. Watching him interrogate a woman who I respected and had counted as a friend over a crime affecting me directly was not something I ever wanted to repeat.

"This is a bad day," Karl said as he took a seat beside me.

"Shouldn't you be in there?" I pointed to the room where Conall was sitting opposite a very irritated Maude.

"The sheriff doesn't want her anger coming down on anybody but him."

That was my Destined Beloved. He always led from the front. It was a quality that I loved about him, but it also scared me to death. Making yourself the sole enemy of one of the most powerful witches in Walker Bay was not a healthy way to lead your life.

"What am I doing here?"

Conall placed the book on the table in front of Maude and tapped it with a finger. "This book was recently found to be in your possession. Considering the events of the past couple of weeks, you can understand my concern.

"Where did you get that?" Maude's voice was pure ice.

My stomach clenched. I had hoped for innocent confusion, maybe some defensiveness of a youthful indiscretion. What we got was aggression.

"This is not good," Karl muttered.

"So, you're familiar with this book," Conall said, his voice not reflecting any emotion at all.

"It was written by a friend of mine," Maude replied, the coldness of her voice contained a warning.

"Isaac Sibley." The sheriff picked up the book and opened it to the dedication page. "He seems to be quite fond of you."

"We were close once."

"When would that have been?"

Maude looked down at the table. "I married very young. Straight out of high school. My mother agreed not to oppose the marriage on the condition I continued my education. My husband stayed here and worked while I went to college."

"That's an unusual arrangement," Conall noted.

Maude laughed humorlessly. "My mother never approved of my husband. It was part of the attraction, I guess. I was a rebellious teenager who was desperate to get out from under my mother's control. I think by encouraging me she was hoping I'd meet somebody else at college."

Conall's eyes flashed with a sudden understanding. "And you met Isaac Sibley."

"He was brilliant and passionate." Maude smiled. "Despite my marriage, I had a crush on him, but it never went anywhere." Maude straightened her shoulders. "I never cheated on my husband."

"Why not?" Conall asked.

Maude sighed. "Isaac had some emotional issues. He had visions, almost as strong as a Seer. He saw a future where a cursebreaker caused an upheaval in the paranormal world. One that destroyed freedoms and the peace between the races. He became obsessed with preventing that future and it changed him." She pointed to the book on the table between them. "He wrote that book as a warning."

"Have you actually read it?" Conall sounded angry, the first time he'd shown emotion in this entire interview. "It goes much further than just a warning. This book advocates cold-blooded murder."

"Hence, the reason it was banned," Maude sighed. "Isaac was never a diplomatic man."

"And yet, you still have a copy," Conall said, finally getting to the point of the interrogation."

Karl and I leaned forward, unwilling to miss a word.

Maude put out her hand and touched the book. "Despite my feelings for Isaac, I loved my husband. We ended up being happily married for a very long time. That book represents a life I almost lived. I realize now it was a life I wouldn't necessarily have been happy with, but the memories make me smile."

"Pity those sentimental memories encourage the killing of innocents."

I winced at the harshness of the sheriff's words.

"Have you had any recent contact with Isaac Sibley?"

The silence in the room was deafening.

"Isaac reached out to me last week. He had become aware of the recent events in Walker Bay and he believed that the vision he had decades ago was coming to fruition."

"What did you tell him?"

"I told him nothing," Maude snapped. "I am not a teenage girl, easily led by my emotions. If there was a problem of that kind in Walker Bay, the coven would take care of it. Outside influences will only exacerbate the problem."

"Do you think he believed you?" Conall asked. "Considering his obvious paranoia and the events of the last few months, it wouldn't take much for him to determine that Walker Bay is a hotbed of cursebreaker conspiracies. He may have decided to investigate himself. Have you seen him in town?"

"No."

"Would you tell me if you had?"

Maude's lips tightened in a straight line. "I have known you since the day you were born. I would think you would know me well enough to accept my word."

"Usually I would," Conall replied, the strain showing in his face. "But these are unusual circumstances. I can't take a chance with Sadie getting hurt again."

Maude straightened in her seat. "Do you really think I would hurt Sadie?"

In contrast to Maude, Conall leaned back in his chair, his posture deceptively casual. "You tell me. Since the announcement of her cursebreaker status, you have been noticeably absent. Not once did you come to the hospital to see her. You haven't checked to see if she's okay. Considering you were the woman who dragged her into this world, I would have thought you'd show a bit more care for her welfare."

"I don't want to see Sadie hurt." Maude seemed to be picking her words carefully. "By the same token, cursebreakers have always been considered dangerous. The Isaac Sibley I knew was a good and gentle man. That vision of the future terrified him enough to write a book that was considered so inflammatory it was banned and all copies were destroyed. It makes me wonder what Sadie is capable of doing and how dangerous she could end up being."

"Are you behind the attempts on her life?" The question was blunt and for a moment Maude looked stunned.

"You believe I would kill Sadie?"

Conall shook his head. "No, I don't, but then I wouldn't think you would be holding a banned book that advocated the continuation of a genocide."

Maude turned towards the window as if she could see through it. "There is a part of me that fears what Sadie is, but I would never hurt her," Maude said clearly. "My loyalty is with my coven leader, and as long as she protects her niece, then I will too."

As far as messages of support, it left a great deal to be desired.

"Very well," Conall replied. "You may go but I may have further questions, so I'll need you to be available."

"Of course, Sheriff Tolan." The sarcasm that rolled out of Maude would have made a teenager proud. "You'll find me at Flora's home if you want to speak to me."

Conall shook his head. "You will no longer be taking care of Flora."

Maude stood up quickly, her eyes flashing with anger. "You cannot keep me from my coven leader."

"We can and we will. Until I have irrefutable proof that you are not a danger to Sadie, you are not going to be in a position of power over the one family member she cares about."

Despite the obvious fury emanating from Maude, Conall stood strong, almost daring her to make a reckless move. The air seemed to crackle with energy. I remembered Maude's abilities as an elemental witch. I hoped that good sense would prevent her from bringing down a lightning bolt to strike the sheriff.

Maude visibly calmed herself and clasped her hands together. I assumed that was to stop her from being tempted to create a storm cloud just above the sheriff's head. "Very well, I will be at home if you have any other questions. I will also be waiting for an apology."

She swept out of the room and it was interesting to see that Karl and Conall had identical expressions on their faces. I guess that's what happened when you had to bring in and interrogate one of your former teachers.

There's a part of me that hopes that she is involved with this," Karl muttered.

"Why would you even say that?" I asked.

"Because if we got it wrong, that woman is going to make us pay for this moment for the rest of our lives."

27

Karl's words were still echoing through my mind later that night as my exhausted brain kept me from getting the deep sleep that my body so desperately needed. On the sheriff's orders he had dropped me off at the house with strict instructions not to leave. I laid in bed agonizing over the fact that someone I had completely trusted may have betrayed me. Part of me refused to believe that Maude would ever do anything like that. But there was a part of me that remembered the look of fear she had given me after Flora had announced my cursebreaker status.

Several hours later I wasn't really sure whether I had got sleep or not. I was in that hyper-vigilant state which worsened when I heard a noise. It took me a few minutes to let go of my fear enough to realize that the only person able to get into my house would be Conall. Nevertheless, I crept quietly down the stairs.

"It's just me," he called up, despite his back being turned.

I was still getting used to werewolf senses. I continued down the stairs and found him hunched over his laptop. The tension rolling off him in waves let me know without words that his day had not been nearly as successful as he had hoped.

"What are you doing?" I murmured, taking the seat next to him as I put a gentle hand on his shoulder.

Conall's head dropped. "I'm trying to find who wants to kill you," he replied, his voice soft. "No matter what I do I seem to be hitting dead ends. The politics involved is putting up roadblocks everywhere I turn." He pulled me onto his lap, burying his head in my shoulder as if he couldn't face me. "I'm missing something, and I have no idea what it is."

I stroked my hand down his back, trying to give him some comfort. "Did you find anything on Isaac Sibley?"

Conall grunted. "My life would be so much easier if he'd become some loner conspiracy theorist living in the woods after his book got banned. Unfortunately, he managed to not only shake off any criticism that was leveled at him by claiming the establishment was trying to stifle alternative ideas, his notoriety made him a popular figure in the witch world. He is now a professor at one of the more prestigious universities and is popular on the speaking circuit. Any attempt to accuse him of being behind the attacks on you will most likely be met with a howl of outrage by his followers. I'm hoping to speak to him in the morning, but a man like that will be very difficult to pin down. I need more time, but I have a bad feeling that I've run out." He lifted his head and those ice blue eyes of his pinned me to the spot. "I know we've discussed this before, but I really think we've reached the point where we need to run and get you somewhere safe. The Assembly is willing to protect you and I have a number of people who can help."

I pulled back from him and stood up, putting some distance between us. "No, I'm not leaving Walker Bay. I will face whatever happens here."

I could tell Conall was trying to control his anger.

"Why won't you even think of running?"

"Because you'll die if I run."

I slapped my hand over my mouth. I hadn't wanted that piece of information to come out like that. To be perfectly honest, I had hoped that I would never let that information out at all, but I needed him to understand that there was no way I was going to risk that.

Conall's eyes widened as understanding slammed into him. "There's been a vision, hasn't there?"

I nodded, unwilling to trust my voice.

"When did you find out?"

"In the hospital." I figured it was only fair that he knew the full truth now I'd let the cat out of the bag. "Flora had a vision that we ran and you were killed trying to protect me. I wasn't going to let that happen."

"Shouldn't that be my decision?" Conall asked, bitterly.

"No," I said simply. "I would have had to live with the consequences of losing you." I swallowed as I felt tears gathering in my eyes. "I won't risk that if there is anything I can do about it. I don't care how mad you get at me."

Conall pulled me into his arms and pressed his lips against my temple. "I am furious with you," he whispered. "Don't ever put my life ahead of yours."

"I can't do that," I replied. "I will always put your life ahead of mine."

Conall dropped his forehead down to mine and looked me in the eyes. "I hate that you did this," he said, "but I understand why."

I knew this was an area where we were never going to be in agreement, so it was probably better to drop the subject completely.

"Any other leads?" I asked, hoping to change to a less contentious subject.

"I've been having a closer look at Rigby."

"I thought he was in some black site that the Assembly took him to." I sat up straight. "Has he escaped?"

Conall shook his head. "No, but I was looking at him and his cause. Who he works with. I was hoping to find some clue as to who was behind him being sent here and if there could be any link to Sibley."

I frowned at the thought. "I wouldn't have thought that was likely. Rigby wanted to recruit me. Based on his book, I have a feeling that Sibley would have a completely different agenda.

"There is a possibility they've crossed paths," Conall mused. "Sibley has been a college professor for decades. That means that he has had access to a lot of people over the years. Just because that book he wrote is banned, doesn't mean that the ideas have gone away. Who knows how many people have been exposed to his beliefs? It just takes one zealot to pick up on an idea before all hell breaks loose."

"So, what do we do next?"

"I have some associates from the Assembly tearing Isaac Sibley's life apart. With any luck they'll shake something loose. For now, he is the best lead that we have." Conall smothered a yawn and I smiled.

"I think it's time for you to come to bed."

He frowned and looked back at the laptop. "I've got to keep on this."

I stood up and held out my hand. "You need sleep. You won't be good to anyone if you're not rested."

I could see the deep need to keep on the hunt. I could also see the fact that he was exhausted.

"I'm not taking no for an answer," I said, softly.

⬆

*T*he languid feeling that spread through my body as I stretched quickly dissipated when I realized that I was alone. It had taken more effort than I had expected to talk Conall into my bed, but I had hoped he'd get a good night's sleep. I sighed when I spotted the piece of paper. I plucked the note off the pillow and read it. There was nothing unexpected. He'd woken early and gone into the office. I wasn't at all surprised. If there was one thing I knew about the sheriff, it was that he was relentless when he was on a mission. I turned my head and looked out of the doors leading to the deck. Another day locked inside. I knew that I had told Conall that I wouldn't be confined anymore, but I was also aware that if he turned the full force of his will onto me I'd probably agree to anything he asked. I wasn't entirely sure that I was happy with that development.

After my shower, I headed downstairs and perused my pantry, trying to muster up some enthusiasm for making myself a decent breakfast. I closed the door with a sigh and opened the refrigerator. I swung the door shut with a little more force than was necessary without grabbing anything. I really wasn't that hungry, and that more than anything should have been a warning sign that I was letting the stress get to me. I opened the pantry again and grabbed a granola bar that I had bought during my ten minutes of healthy living that had happened several weeks ago. As I chewed on it, I remembered the reason why I rarely ate these foods. I was working on some grains that had got stuck in my teeth when my phone rang.

Recognizing Tilda's number, I answered with a smile on my face. Before I could say anything Tilda's panicked voice came through the line.

"Someone put a curse on Flora!" she yelled, the words barely coherent. "There are all these little things wriggling over her. I don't know what to do."

I was already grabbing my keys and heading out the door when I finally managed to get a word in. "I'm on my way. Do not touch her. Do not go anywhere near her."

I steeled myself against the anger flowing through me at the thought of Flora being the victim of a curse. Again. It had taken ages for Flora to recover from the curse placed on her by one of her closest friends. She was already weak from the spell creating the shield around my house. If I wasn't able to remove the curse in time, it could kill her. I got in my car and put the keys in the ignition. I turned my head slightly as I yanked on my seatbelt and something flickered in my peripheral vision. I didn't have a chance for my brain to process what I saw before I felt a sharp prick in my neck and a wave of pain surged through my entire body. It lasted for what I thought was hours but could have only been a few seconds, and then the pain stopped. I would like to say that I sprang into action against my assailant, but the truth was that I was struggling not to lose the contents of my stomach, my brain felt like it had checked out, and my body felt so sore that the thought of moving made me want to scream.

"Now you are going to drive," a voice behind me whispered. "I've given you a small taste of what this thing is capable of. If you try to do anything to bring attention to yourself, I will put this to the back of your neck with the prongs on either side of your spine, and I will hold it there for five minutes while electricity passes through you until your nervous system shuts down."

I wished I'd paid more attention when Pike had been waxing lyrical about his stun gun. I wasn't sure if the person in my backseat could do what they were saying, but I wasn't very keen on finding out the truth in my driveway. I swallowed, almost choking on my saliva as my throat seemed to have closed over.

"My aunt has been cursed. Please let me go to her."

The low chuckle in the back seat chilled me. "Your aunt is fine. Your friend, however, is very suggestible. She really needs to stop believing everything she sees."

That was when it hit me. I'd been so panicked by the thought of Flora being cursed that I hadn't given a thought to the fact that Tilda had claimed to have seen the tendrils which were the hallmark of a curse. As a cursebreaker I was the only one who could see them. If I still had full control of my body, I would have kicked myself. That's what happens when you don't stop to think before reacting.

"Start the car," the voice said.

This was going to be interesting. I wasn't yet sure whether I had full control of my body and I was going to be in charge of a hunk of metal which was temperamental on the best of days. I turned the key and my car started without a hitch. I should have known that the one time I wanted it to not start would be the one time it started perfectly.

"What now?"

"Head towards Harstone Manor."

This was beginning to make sense. I glanced at the

rearview mirror, but the gray balaclava prevented me from seeing which of my loving family was kidnapping me. "Who are you?"

"I don't think that's something you need to know just yet."

I tried to place the voice, but I couldn't. It was pitched low and I couldn't even tell if it was male or female to narrow down the field.

I looked around as I pulled out into the street. Everyone who knew me, knew that I was supposed to be confined and protected by an overenthusiastic sheriff. I had to hope that someone would stop and think it was weird that I was driving around town. Unfortunately, it looked like everyone had decided to sleep in this morning. The streets were deserted. I kept wishing a cop car would pull up behind me but despite what Tilda seemed to think, there wasn't a police car hiding behind every tree. I started experimenting by lightly tapping on the brakes hoping that if someone was looking they'd at least think that something strange was going on. I froze when I felt the stun gun being pressed against my skin.

"I suggest you stop doing that. I can guarantee that if we get pulled over I will not hesitate to do you as much damage as humanly possible before anyone can rescue you. You ruined my life. I will be only too happy to end yours."

So much for that plan. As we continued driving, I tried to work out what had happened to my magical abilities. Despite not liking to use the darkness that was a side effect from breaking curses I was willing to make an exception when my life was in danger, but no matter how much I tried to reach into myself and tap into the power, I came up with nothing. I felt a moment of panic. Without that power I was at the mercy of someone who I had a feeling had already tried to kill me twice. It looked like I was going to need to cast my mind back to all the ways my mother had tried to teach me to protect myself, way back before I knew anything about witches, werewolves and the ogre that I really wished was on patrol this morning. If I survived, I was seriously going to have a chat to the sheriff about the lack of police on the roads. Even one would have pulled me over by now.

"Turn right here on this road."

We weren't quite at the manor, but I knew we were on the property. To call this a road was definitely overstating things. The torn-up track was rarely used, and my car was definitely not built for off-road driving. I could hear my attacker grunting as we hit a particularly deep pothole. The steady feel of prongs on my neck told me the jolt had not been enough to distract them from their goal. We drove along the track for several minutes before a small building came into view.

"Stop here."

I braked a little harder than was necessary and was given a quick jolt from the stun gun in retaliation. The pain shot through me and I was barely given an opportunity to recover before another shot, longer this time, was put into my system. By the time I'd recovered enough to move again my kidnapper was pulling open my door and dragging me out. Now that I could see them properly, I could tell from their size that I was dealing with a woman, but I was in no condition to put up a fight. She opened the door to the cabin and gave me a push, sending me sprawling to the floor.

The door was slammed shut behind us and she stalked towards me. I scrambled backwards, my body moving sluggishly as I tried to find anything that would help me.

She jammed the stun gun into my side and gave me another shot of electricity. I tried to be strong, but I heard myself whimpering as the pain grew to be too much and I couldn't move. She grabbed hold of me and hauled me up onto a chair, wrenching my hands behind my back and tying them together.

By the time I began to feel like I no longer needed to scream, I was realizing that there was nothing that I could do and I was completely at her mercy. Mercy which she obviously didn't have.

↑

While I tried to work out if there was any way I could get out of this predicament, my attacker took off the balaclava.

"Lorelei?"

If I'd had to lay bets on which one of the Harstone clan would be the one to try to kill me, my stepsister would have come close to the bottom of the list. Although, to be honest, considering how little I knew them, I guess she was just as likely a candidate as any of the others. The question was, why?

"So, are you the one who's been trying to kill me?" I spat out some blood from when I bit my tongue during one of the several times she'd tried to electrocute me.

"Of course, I am. You think there's more than one person who wants you dead?"

I lifted my shoulder. "I'm sure there are dozens of people who want to kill off a cursebreaker. I just found out about a man who's written an instruction manual on the subject. My question is, why did you act on it?"

"I thought you killed the man I love."

It took a couple of seconds before my brain narrowed down who she was talking about. "Rigby? You're in love with Liam Rigby?"

This was all starting to make some sort of sense.

"I saw the video. I thought you'd killed him."

"Well, I didn't," I said. "So, your whole revenge thing is pointless. Now if you let me go, we'll just forget this entire incident ever happened."

Yeah, I knew that was a longshot, but I figured you never know unless you try. Considering her actions, I was pretty sure that Lorelei wasn't playing with a complete deck. Sometimes those people surprise you.

Unfortunately, Lorelei was not in a surprising mood. "You can go when Liam is free."

"Excuse me?"

"I'm willing to swap you for my boyfriend. If the Assembly is so keen to keep you alive, they'll be only too happy to agree."

This was bad. So very, very bad. Now I had two choices. I could try to convince her that the Assembly was not going to release a murderer purely to save me, which I figured to be the most likely scenario. Or, I could play along and encourage her belief in the viability of her plan. I had a pretty good idea which of those options at least gave me a chance of surviving the next hour.

"Why haven't you got your family to lobby the Assembly," I asked, hoping to keep her attention off any thoughts she had of hitting me with that stun gun again.

Lorelei grimaced. "My mother doesn't approve of Liam. She doesn't know that we're together. Liam says we should wait to tell her when he's in a better position."

I looked at the girl in front of me and wanted to scream. I couldn't believe my life was forfeit because of some frustrated romance.

"I was going through Liam's computer the night you attacked him. I saw what you did to him," she said in an accusatory tone.

She was going through his computer. That sounded like a healthy relationship.

"Did you by any chance see the part where he kidnapped my friend and was slowly strangling her to death?"

Lorelei started pacing. "He was doing what needed to be done. Cursebreakers cannot be allowed to live. It's the law. He is a magister, an honorable man."

I snorted. "Your honorable man wasn't interested in killing me. He was trying to convince me to work with him. His loyalty is to someone who wants to use my power."

Lorelei shook her head. "That's not true. He's seen the vision. He knows what the cursebreaker will bring."

"What vision?

"Professor Sibley shared his vision with us. He knows what will happen if you are allowed to survive."

I shook my head, trying desperately to clear the fog that seemed to encompass it.

"I hate to be the one to burst your bubble, but I have no reason to lie to you. Rigby threatened my friend to try to get me to work with him. I'm not saying it was the smartest way he could have approached me. In fact, it was the opposite of the smartest way to get me to do what he wanted."

"You lie," she snarled.

I knew at that moment that nothing I said was going to get through. Reason and logic had exited the building and I was left with an emotional woman with a very bad case of relationship delusion.

My eyes flickered to the window behind her and I saw movement. I focused and was surprised to see my cousin, Malin, at the window. I wasn't quite sure if I should get my hopes up at this stage. I still wasn't certain where all of the

Harstones fell on the whole killing cursebreakers issue. I was really hoping Malin was more of the live and let live kind of person.

Unfortunately, Lorelei had noticed my distraction and her eyes followed mine just as Malin ducked down. Wanting to keep Lorelei's attention on me I started shaking my head and clicking my tongue.

Her head snapped back. "What are you doing?"

"I'm appreciating the irony of the fact that you became an assassin because you didn't have the guts to tell your family who you were in love with. And not just any assassin. Trust me when I say that I saw a piece of your soul in that curse you did on the explosives attached to my house. There is something sick and twisted going on inside you." I knew I was pushing a woman who would quite happily kill me, but I just felt like I had to keep going. Anything to give Malin the time to do the right thing and get some help. "It's not surprising," I continued, "Liam Rigby smothered a dying man in his sleep and from what I heard about his interrogation he admitted he enjoyed doing it." I cocked my head to the side as if I was asking an innocuous question. "Was it the darkness in him that called to you?"

I saw the fist heading my way, but I was too sluggish to dodge it. Fortunately, the blow was glancing. Just like everything else she had tried. An attempt at being strong that didn't quite come off the way she intended.

"You know that he was involved with Tilda," I said, in the hope of keeping her unbalanced. "Seems he wasn't quite as devoted to you as you were to him."

Lorelei clenched her fists and I could see she wanted to hit me again, but she was wary. Her attempts at killing me had been brutal, but you could see that this wasn't something that came naturally, considering her privileged upbringing. Despite that, I could tell she was learning fast.

"Why are you trying to make me angry?"

I was hoping she wouldn't see through my clumsy attempts to distract her. It looked like I wasn't quite as clever as I thought I was.

"Do you really think you can trade me for a murderer and just walk away and live happily ever after?"

I was surprised to find I was genuinely curious to see what her answer would be.

"You couldn't know what it is to love so deeply."

I wasn't going to touch that one.

"Liam is my life. I need him."

Sympathy flashed through me. I was going to blame it on the multiple times she had stunned me.

I couldn't say who was more shocked when the front door to the cabin was pushed open and my grandmother was standing there. I wondered who she was here to help.

"This is unfortunate," she stated. She moved into the cabin and stopped, her eyes not wavering from the scene in front of her. "You always have such hopes for your grandchildren. You know they can't possibly live up to them, but you hope." She shook her head. "It's so disappointing when they inevitably don't live up to those hopes."

I was going to blame it on the stun gun and my foggy brain, but I was still not sure whose side she was on.

Lorelei stepped back and grabbed a handful of my hair, wrenching my head back and jamming the stun gun against my neck again. Despite knowing it was not going to help me at all, I tensed in preparation for the next jolt.

"I would suggest you think very carefully about your next move," Collette warned Lorelei, giving me an inkling of hope. "I have treated you like family since the day your mother married my son, but make no mistake, Sadie is my blood. I will not hesitate to destroy you to protect her."

"How can you?" Lorelei cried out, her hand shaking. "She's an abomination. She must be destroyed."

"That is for the Conclave to decide, not you."

And once again I was back to wondering if Collette was actually on my side.

Lorelei straightened as if she was remembering her original plan. "If they give Liam back to me, they can have her."

Collette gave her a pitying look. "Liam Rigby has made his own path. Nothing is going to change his fate. Frankly, I don't understand what you ever saw in that boy. There was always something not quite right with him."

I could feel Lorelei's grip on my hair tighten. If Collette was trying to talk her down, she was doing a lousy job. Unfortunately, I was not in a position to do anything to help my situation. To know that my life completely depended on a woman that I didn't trust was a sobering thought.

I felt another yank on my hair and I closed my eyes, preparing myself for the jolt of pain I knew was coming. My eyes snapped back open as I felt the stun gun being dragged against the skin of my neck and then being pulled away. I looked up to find the sheriff had a hold of Lorelei's arms and was pushing her to the ground. I had no idea where he had come from, but I was never so happy to see anybody in my entire life.

"You okay?" he growled as he pulled away the stun gun and handcuffed her hands behind her back.

I shook my head, unable to voice what I was feeling.

"Take her," he barked as he shoved a screaming Lorelei at Deputy Iversen who had come from the same place the sheriff had.

Karl bundled her out of the cabin leaving me with Conall and Collette, both of them looking at me as if they were expecting me to fall apart. They were right. Other times when I had faced dangerous situations, I had at least felt like

I could attempt to defend myself and go down fighting. This time, I had discovered what it was to be completely defenseless. I really didn't like the feeling at all. Conall stepped behind me and cut the ties around my wrist. As I straightened my arms, I couldn't stop myself from whimpering.

"I've got you, babe," Conall murmured as he leaned down and plucked me out of the chair.

I didn't argue. I felt so defeated and I hated it. He held me to his chest and as he strode out of the cabin, I lifted my head.

"Thank you," I whispered to Collette as we passed her.

She nodded her head. "You're my granddaughter," she said simply as if that was the only important thing I needed to know.

For the first time I found comfort in that statement.

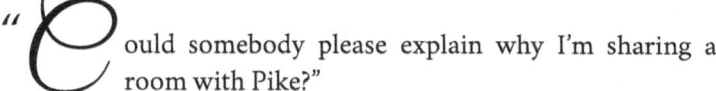

"Could somebody please explain why I'm sharing a room with Pike?"

Dr Collias smiled, which couldn't be a good thing. "We thought it would be a learning experience for him to have to live with a victim of a stun gun. Please feel free to describe in excruciating detail the effects you're feeling."

I would have thought that the number of times I had walked across the threshold of his clinic—mostly to help the good doctor heal his patients—would entitle me to a bit of preferential treatment. Unfortunately, that didn't seem to be the case.

"Trust me, I'm not happy about this either," grumbled Pike.

When Conall had rescued me from the cabin, he had wasted no time in getting me to the clinic to be checked. After Collias had managed to convince my Destined Beloved that the only permanent damage from repeated jolts from a stun gun were a couple of nasty burns on my neck which would heal in time, I'd finally talked him into leaving me while he did his job and unraveled the mess that was Lorelei

Blackwood. He hadn't been thrilled at my insistence that he get back to work, and I had a feeling that my new roommate was his way of voicing his displeasure. At first I had been fine with the arrangement, but it had been a long day.

I rubbed the back of my neck, wincing as my bandages caught on the burns and looked over at my roommate. "You're the expert. Why wasn't I able to defend myself using magic?"

Pike grimaced. "Yeah, stun guns have a bad effect on witches and their magic as well as werewolves. There's a reason why it's my favorite weapon. It's a great equalizer."

"You could have told me that," I said. "If I'd known, maybe it wouldn't have been as bad. I could have had a plan in place."

"I did tell you that," he said with a calmness that didn't really suit him.

"No," I replied. "You told me it messed with werewolves. I distinctly remember because your enjoyment of the pain it caused gave me real concerns about you. At no time did you mention it could scramble my brains and take away any chance I had to defend myself."

"I was trying to be tactful," he retorted. "I didn't think our relationship was ready for that kind of a revelation. If I'd told you how badly a stun gun messes up witches, you might have felt uncomfortable around me." He huffed. "And I am not giving up my favorite weapon. I don't care how freaked out you are."

"I want to leave." I turned my focus to the doctor who was watching the two of us with a slightly amused look on his face.

"I'm not letting you out of here without an escort," Collias replied.

As if in answer to my prayers an exhausted looking sheriff entered the room.

"You ready to get out of here?"

"Yes, definitely."

I hopped off the bed and was gratified that the room only spun slightly. I could work with that.

"How come she gets to escape and I'm still stuck here?" Pike complained.

"Would you believe we would miss your sparkling personality?" Collias replied, not looking up from the paperwork.

"You don't lie well, Doc," retorted Pike.

Collias raised his head and smiled. "Yes, I do. I just choose not to employ that particular skill with you."

"You're staying in here until the doctor signs off on your release." I could tell from Conall's tone that he was not in the mood to humor anyone. "Try not to irritate the staff too much."

Pike straightened and managed to look affronted. "I have been the perfect patient."

"On the short walk from the waiting area I've had four staff members begging me to take you out of here," the sheriff replied. "None of them said it was because you'd been such a perfect patient."

Pike huffed. "It's not my fault they can't handle their job."

"Just take it easy with them," Conall sighed.

I walked over to Pike and dropped a kiss on his head. "Be nice."

"It's like you don't know me at all."

"I want to see Flora," I announced as we hopped in the car.

"I'm not sure…"

"Maybe I need to rephrase that. I need to see Flora."

Conall studied me for a second. "Flora it is."

It didn't take us long to reach Flora's house and Tilda was waiting outside.

"I'm so sorry," she said. "I was sure I was seeing those tendrils you keep talking about on Flora. I could have touched them. I should have thought it through. I shouldn't have panicked."

I put my hand on her arm. "None of us knew that Lorelei had the ability to create images. I reacted without thinking too. She was depending on our feelings for Flora and she was right."

"Can we have this conversation inside the house where it's safer?"

I could feel the tension radiating from Conall as his head swiveled. I noticed that he had placed himself at my back, between me and anyone who wanted to do me harm.

"Of course," I murmured as I gave Tilda a slight nudge in the direction of the house.

Once inside I found Flora laying on the couch, looking a lot more pale and fragile than I was comfortable with. I sat on the ground next to her and stroked her hair. "Are you okay?"

She gave me a watery smile. "I should be asking you that." She raised her hand to touch the bandage at my neck.

"It's nothing," I assured her. "Just a couple of minor burns. They'll heal in no time."

"I'm sorry you were betrayed by a member of your family."

I shook my head. "You're my family. They are just some people I met recently. I have no loyalty to them and no expectations of loyalty from them." I looked around the room. "I think the only surprise was which one of them was trying to kill me."

Conall cleared his throat. "I hate to be the one to defend the Harstones, but I don't know how well the operation to rescue you would have gone without Collette's help. And your cousin was the one who raised the alarm."

I frowned up at him. "Why did you have Collette come through the door?" That had been bothering me. Based on previous experience, I would have expected the sheriff to have led the charge to rescue me.

"I was playing the odds that Lorelei was unstable," Conall replied.

That was a good guess.

"We needed a distraction that would hold her attention while Iversen and I came through the back door," Conall continued. "After your cousin started calling for help, we had a few people outside. We just needed a way to get inside that didn't endanger you." He shrugged. "Seeing as nobody's really sure where Collette's loyalties lie, I figured she would be the best one to distract Lorelei."

I couldn't argue with the results. I rubbed my chest where I still felt pain from where the arrow had entered. For some reason it was really hurting today. Maybe it was acting as a reminder, telling me how lucky I had been. I had felt sure when Lorelei had led me into that cabin that nobody was going to find us.

"Why was Malin near the cabin?"

"Supposedly dumb luck," Conall said, although I could tell he wasn't necessarily sold on that explanation. "According to her, she enjoys walking through the woods on the Harstone property. She was passing by when the two of you arrived. We're fortunate that she acted quickly and called for help. By the time I got there, Collette was preparing to storm the place. There was no way we were keeping her out of it." He shook his head. "Lorelei really had no clue what she was doing. That place was not defensible at all. We're lucky she had more enthusiasm for what she was doing than competence."

I rubbed my chest again. Her enthusiasm came very close to killing me. I wasn't quite so willing to discount it.

"What's going to happen with her?"

"She's going to be charged with attempted murder."

"Of a cursebreaker," I reminded him. "Can she be charged when I'm living under a death sentence anyway?"

Conall looked grim. "This is one of the few times when operating under more than one legal system works. It doesn't matter about the Conclave and their precepts. Assembly laws come first in Walker Bay. That means she will be charged with attempted murder and kidnapping. If her goal was to get her lover back, she failed in the most spectacular way possible. She will most likely not be seeing him for the rest of her life."

I was about to ask another question when there was a knock at the door. Conall strode over and opened it. I could tell from his stance that the visitor wasn't entirely welcome.

"I wish to see my granddaughter."

I dropped my head at the demand. I was impressed that Collette had waited this long before requiring my attention. Conall looked at me and I nodded. He stepped back and Collette walked into the house. I was surprised to see her accompanied by Maude.

"The Conclave held an emergency session. They've repealed the precept that orders death for all cursebreakers."

My mouth dropped open at Collette's announcement. Of all the consequences of our decision to go public, I hadn't ever let myself hope that this would happen.

"How...?"

"I called an emergency meeting of the Conclave and put forward in the strongest terms possible that enforcing a death sentence on a witch for no reason other than the way they were born was not a good look in these modern times," she replied.

Of all the reasons for lifting the arbitrary threat to my life I had hoped it would be the immorality of the law rather than public relations being the motivating factor. However, beggars couldn't be choosers, so I was going to accept the ruling of the Conclave.

"Your stepmother wished me to convey her deepest apologies for the actions of your stepsister. She wants you to know that Lorelei's actions in no way represent the feelings of the Blackwood family toward you. She believes strongly that Lorelei was an impressionable young woman who came under the malevolent influence of Professor Isaac Sibley and Magister Liam Rigby. She hopes this incident does not affect your developing relationship with your father."

Considering there was no developing relationship with Jasper, we were all good on that front.

I nodded tightly. "I wanted to thank you for your assistance. I wasn't sure how I was going to get out of there. When you came through the door, I knew I was safe."

Considering I was still questioning where Collette's truly allegiances lay that was a little white lie, but she deserved something.

She stood there quietly for a few seconds as if deciding what she should say next.

"Your family is here to stay," she said quietly. "I realize, considering everything that's happened, that may be hard for you to believe. We want to be a part of your life." She leaned down and cupped my face. "You are my legacy, Sadie. I will not let that go without a fight."

I was not comforted by that statement, and a quick glance at Conall showed he was trying very hard not to react as if it was a threat.

Collette straightened. "When you are fully recovered, we will talk." She gave Flora a tight nod and headed for the front door.

Once she'd left, I opened my mouth to say something but closed it again when I saw Conall shake his head as he frowned at Maude.

"I know you don't trust me," she said, her gaze fixed on me. "I haven't reacted well to the announcement of your curse breaking abilities, and I'm sorry for that. I wish I could say that I'm able to accept you being a cursebreaker." She glanced at Tilda and I could see her granddaughter's disappointed expression was causing her a great deal of pain. "But I think that there are going to be consequences here that none of us are seeing. We need to be prepared for them."

Flora pulled herself to a seating position. "I never thought I would see the day you bowed to prejudice and hysteria." Her voice trembled. "Until you can see past Sadie's ability, I don't see a place for you at my side."

Maude's eyes glistened and I could see that losing Flora's faith was cutting her deeply.

She bowed her head. "As you wish."

She didn't make eye contact with any of us as she left. I reached out a hand to Tilda, certain that this was hurting my friend.

Tilda wiped her eyes. "This isn't her," she insisted. "I have never known her to react like this to anybody who didn't deserve it."

"Talk to her," I urged. "Find out what she's so afraid of." I took in a deep breath. "For all we know, she could be right. None of us is an expert on cursebreakers. We're all learning on the fly. Just because we don't agree with what she's saying doesn't mean her concerns aren't valid."

Tilda nodded. "I need to talk to her. Maybe if I could understand where her fears are coming from I might be able to..." Her voice drifted off as she realized the difficulty involved in trying to change a person's deeply held beliefs. She blinked fiercely. "She's my grandmother. I have to try."

"Of course you do," Flora said, a soothing tone in her voice. "I would never ask you to make a choice between us."

I nodded my head in agreement. I knew her stance against Maude was hurting Flora, but the situation would destroy Tilda if we let it.

"Do you need me to stay?" Tilda asked.

I shook my head. "I'll take care of her," I replied. "You do whatever you need to do. We'll be fine." I stood up and gave her a hug. She walked out with her shoulders stooped as if the weight of the world was on them.

"This shouldn't be happening," I said. "This has the potential to tear us apart."

Flora grasped my hand and pulled me down beside her. "Every family goes through rough times. I'm not just talking about Maude and Tilda. This town is a family, full of strong personalities. We'll disagree and argue at times, but I truly believe we will come together when it counts."

I certainly hoped so.

"What do you think of Collette's news?" I asked.

Flora looked concerned but Conall shrugged. "I'm not overly surprised," he said. "There are some moderate elements getting into the Conclave. Add that to the embarrassment that a member of one of the more important families in the witch world going off the rails and actually trying to assassinate you. I would say they are trying to get ahead of the bad publicity and make a gesture of peace."

"Does this mean that I'm safe?" I could barely believe it and when I looked over at Conall the sense of relief I had been feeling stuttered and died. "I'll never be safe."

"I still don't trust them," he sighed, "but then I don't think there is anything that they could do that would make me trust them. Lorelei is insisting that going after you was her idea alone. According to her, Isaac Sibley knew nothing of what she was doing but I can't shake the feeling that he is a threat. However, without any evidence there is nothing I can do about him. It isn't illegal to have unpopular views."

"So, what do we do now?"

Conall pulled me up into his arms. "We keep you safe," he growled. "We gather our allies and we prepare for whatever is heading our way."

I wrapped my arms around his waist and squeezed as I tried to ignore the look of fear in Flora's eyes. I had a feeling that no matter what we did, we were never going to be prepared for what came next.

ABOUT THE AUTHOR

Leonie Gant started her writing career at the age of ten when she stuffed notes in her pencil case full of ideas for mysteries that Nancy Drew and the Hardy Boys should really have been solving. After years of watching mysteries play out in her head she decided that writing them down was the best way to deal with them.

In her life away from writing, she is a voracious reader with not nearly enough time to make her way through all the books she wants to read. She also enjoys bushwalking, sewing and chocolate, possibly not in that order.

To find out more about Leonie Gant and her books

www.leoniegant.com

DISCOVER OTHER TITLES BY LEONIE GANT

The Harstone Legacy

Curse the Dark

Curse the Soul

Curse the Heart

Curse the Past

Curse the Truth

Not in Hollywood

Not Famous in Hollywood

Not Happily Married in Hollywood

Not Talented in Hollywood

Not Wanted in Hollywood

Not Suspicious in Hollywood

Not Forgotten in Hollywood

www.ingramcontent.com/pod-product-compliance
Lightning Source LLC
Chambersburg PA
CBHW031311120626
46554CB00001BA/365

9780648981114